HIGHTAIL IT TO KINSEY FALLS

GAYLE LEESON

Hightail it to Kinsey Falls by Gayle Leeson
ISBN: 978-0-9741090-7-7

Grace Abraham Publishing

Chapter One

A S MILLIE WALKED OUT of the Community Center, she made a mental list of the things she needed from the grocery store. She didn't need much: coffee pods, dishwashing detergent, tea pods—she certainly didn't need a baby possum.

But there it was, crouching in the sun at the side of the walk. At least, that's what she *thought* it was. She stepped over into the grass and leaned closer. The gray and white creature with the tiny pink paws and tail looked as if it were trying to disappear into the ground. It opened its wide mouth and emitted a harmless little hiss at her.

Yep. It was a possum.

"Oh, poor baby." Millie saw no sign of its mother or any siblings, but there were too many dogs and cats around to leave the poor thing to fend for itself. She rifled through her purse until she found her makeup bag. She emptied the bag into the purse, sat the purse on the ground beside her, and proceeded to use the now-empty canvas bag to capture the baby possum. Once it was inside the bag, she quickly zipped it closed, leaving a small breathing hole.

Millie grabbed her purse and hurried back into the building. The pet shop was located right beside Nothin' But Knit, and she hoped Jade and Terri wouldn't spot her. How in the world would Millie explain to her granddaughter that she had a possum in her makeup bag?

The bell over the door of Hightail It! Pet Supply and Grooming jingled when Millie went inside.

"Be right with you," a male voice called.

"Hurry, please!" Millie placed her purse on the counter so she could hold the cosmetic bag with both hands. The possum didn't appear to be moving. She'd like to have unzipped the bag just a bit more, but she'd prefer to wait until the professional arrived.

A muscular young man came out of the stockroom with a fifty-pound bag of dog food on his shoulder. He eased the bag onto the floor and smiled at Millie. "Someone called and requested we have this bag ready for pickup today. Was that you?"

This guy was really handsome. Thick, wavy dark hair with a bit of a curl to it, deep chocolate-colored eyes, excellent build shown off to perfection in a white tee shirt and nicely fitting jeans... Had Jade met him?

Millie realized she was staring and smiled. "Nope. Not me."

He returned her smile. "What can I do for you then?"

"I have a... Well, I was going to my car, and I found this...this...." She held the makeup bag toward the young man.

He took it gingerly. "What've you got in here—a bird?"

"It's a...possum."

That sent his eyebrows skyward. "Huh. Well, let's see what we can do. Be right back."

He carefully put the bag on the counter before sprinting back to the stockroom. He returned with a small, square box with high enough sides that, hopefully, the possum wouldn't escape and run amok in the shop.

Handsome held the bag inside the box and slowly unzipped it.

"Hmm…" He gently turned the bag onto its side and dumped the tiny body into the box.

As soon as the young man moved his head, Millie peered inside. "Oh, no! Is it dead? Did I kill it?"

"No. I believe what you're seeing is called tonic immobility." He held up the makeup bag by his index finger and thumb. "I do think you're gonna want to replace this, though. Your new buddy left you a not-so-pleasant present."

"Ugh...yeah. Could you get rid of that bag for me?"

He laughed. "Sure. I'll throw it in our dumpster out back." In the meantime, he double bagged it. "I'm Caleb, by the way."

"Millie." She sighed. "Bless its heart—I didn't mean to scare it. It's just a baby. I was trying to mount a rescue."

"I know." He seemed to shrug off her bringing a possum into his shop as if it were an everyday occurrence.

"Do you live upstairs?" Millie asked.

"I do," he said. "You?"

"Yep. Other side of the hall from you, I'm sure."

"Nah! Really? How'd you get stuck over there with the golden oldies?" He grinned.

"Just lucky, I guess." She looked around the pet shop. She didn't have any pets of her own and had never been inside. "This is a nice place. Is it yours?"

"No, I'm just working here while getting my graduate degree in urban and regional planning."

"That sounds..." She shrugged. "It sounds confusing. What is it?"

"It's basically coming up with stuff like this Community Center," he said. "This is the type of designing I want to do. Take things in danger of being discarded and make them useful and new again."

The Kinsey Falls Living and Retail Community Center was the brainchild of an innovative real estate developer who had taken a dying mall and had turned it into a community that catered to two specific groups—seniors and young professionals. The upstairs had been converted to micro-apartments with the "golden oldies" on the left side and the YPs on the right. The retail spaces downstairs were designed to appeal to both groups as well as to the general public. There were common areas both upstairs and down, and community gardens were located at the right and left sides of the building.

"Don't let some of those *golden oldies* hear you say that. They'd take it as a challenge."

"You think?"

"I *know*. I imagine there are several of the women who'd try to give *Mrs*. Caleb a run for her money."

He arched a brow. "Are you fishing, Millie?"

"A little," she admitted. "My single granddaughter owns the knitting shop right next door to you. Pretty redhead. Have you noticed her in here?"

"I haven't. And I'm sure I'd remember a pretty redhead. You think I should take up knitting?"

"Maybe you should. It's very relaxing…or so they tell me."

"You don't knit?"

"Heavens, no." She grinned. "Maybe I will one day…when I'm a golden oldie." She nodded at the box. "How long before we know if Baby Possum is alive or in--intoxicated or whatever you called it?"

"Tonic immobility. It could last up to four hours."

"Goodness! It'll take that long to determine whether it's alive or not?"

"Hopefully not," Caleb said. "In the meantime, I'll call the one of the local veterinarians to see how we should proceed."

"Well, if the poor possum is still alive and the vet will treat it, I'll take it to the animal hospital." She shrugged. "I feel responsible for little…Perry."

"Perry?"

"Yeah. That sounds like a good unisex name, don't you think?"

Caleb laughed. "Perry the possum, it is."

Millie took a card out of her purse. The black and gold card had *Millicent Fairchild* in bold, elegant letters in the middle of the card and her cell phone number in a smaller font below her name. She'd taken an online printing company up on their offer of free business cards after she'd gotten her phone. She handed the card to Caleb. "Please let me know when Perry wakes up."

"I will, Millie. And I'll let you know what the vet says too."

"Thanks." She smiled to herself as she left the store. Caleb was handsome, kind, educated…he could be a great match for Jade. Millie wasn't thinking about happily forever after for Jade, like her daughter Fiona was, but she could see that Jade was lonely. A little male companionship would do her granddaughter good.

* * *

Jade put the blue cat carrier onto the hot pink countertop at Nothin' But Knit and let Mocha out into the shop. Mocha, a seal point Himalayan, was a fixture in the store. He strolled out of the carrier, bumped Terri on the chin with his large head, and hopped down onto the oak hardwood floor to wind around Jade's feet. Jade sat the carrier beneath the counter.

It was already seventy-five degrees on this Saturday morning, and Jade was glad the Community Center had excellent air conditioning. Terri, Jade's business partner and best friend since middle school, was making sure the shop was tidy before unlocking the doors. The shop—and in fact, the entire Kinsey Falls Living and Retail Community Center—had only been open for a few weeks. The grand opening celebration was being held a week from today.

"You're going to teach this loom class, aren't you?" Terri asked, brows furrowing together over wide brown eyes. "You know I don't do great with kids."

"Aw, come on," Jade said. "This experience would be good for you."

"No, it wouldn't."

Jade laughed as her grandmother Millie waltzed into the shop and did a three-sixty spin.

"How do y'all like my new duds?" She wore a black, pink, and white floral print maxi skirt with a fuchsia V-neck tee. Like Jade, Millie had once been a redhead, but now her hair was a silvery white.

"That's a gorgeous outfit," Terri said. "But I thought you had a moratorium on new clothes for the time being."

The moratorium was because the micro-apartments upstairs didn't have a great deal of storage space.

"I do. And the other gals do too. That's why some of us got together and decided to host a swap meet in the atrium. We're going to have one each month and trade off," Millie said. "And not just clothing but scarves, bags, and jewelry too."

"How fun!" Jade kissed Millie's cheek. "My smart, sexy grandma."

"You got that right. You gals are welcome to come to the next one. We're trying to get as many people involved as possible." She smoothed out her skirt. "Now, what were you saying would be a good experience for Terri? Y'all know how I hate missing stuff."

"Yep, Grandma, you've got serious FOMO."

"Fear of missing out," Terri explained to a bewildered Millie. "She's trying to get me to teach the tween girls' loom class."

"One girl's mom booked the class as part of her daughter's birthday celebration." Jade placed eight looms on the counter. "She bought each one a loom and the yarn to make a scarf."

"Gee whiz. When your mother was little, we just had a cake," said Millie. "When *you* were little, your mother sent everybody off with goodie bags full of candy and cheap toys. Today, the moms are buying looms and yarn for whole parties full of kids? Sounds like an expensive takeaway to me."

"It's all about the experiences," Jade said. "Sure, people today want *stuff,* but they want experiences even more. Well, you get it, Grandma, or else you wouldn't live at the Community Center."

6

Millie shrugged. "Experience, my foot. I don't see why they can't share a loom."

"For one thing, they can't all make a scarf on one loom at the same time. And for another, they can't share a loom because that's bad for our business," Terri pointed out.

"She's got you there, Grandma." Jade carried the looms into the knitting room and spaced them out evenly on the large, round table. The table had been a flea-market find and had a distressed white finish. The armless chairs were upholstered in pink-and-purple paisley.

"Also, there's no way the girls can finish their scarves in the allotted time. They'll need to take their looms and yarn home to complete them," Jade called from the knitting room. She ran her palms down the sides of her jeans as she returned to the main part of the shop. "What are your plans for the rest of the day?"

"After I leave here, I'm going to pick up a few essentials at the grocery store. When I get back and put my groceries away, I'll go to the pet shop and check on Perry."

"Who's Perry?" Terri asked.

"Perry is a…a baby…animal…that I found outside this morning and took over to the pet shop. Have you gals met Caleb? He works in the pet shop and is absolutely dreamy."

"Wait, who are Perry and Caleb again?" Jade asked.

Millie blew out a breath. "Weren't you listening? Caleb is the gorgeous guy who works at the pet shop. He's a real sweetheart too."

"And you met him how?" Jade frowned. Her grandmother didn't even own a pet. What was she doing visiting the pet shop?

"I met him when I took Perry, the rescued animal, to him," Millie said. "He's helping me make sure Perry is safe."

Jade ran a hand across her brow. "And what kind of animal is Perry?"

Millie pursed her lips. "Perry is a possum."

Terri laughed. "Perry, the possum! That's cute!"

"Grandma! You picked up a freaking possum? Are you out of your mind?"

"I didn't pick up the possum…exactly. I kinda scooped it into my makeup bag."

"Ewww!" Jade threw both hands up to the sides of her head "Grandma, that's *nasty*! You've got to throw all that makeup away—"

"Jade, please. I certainly didn't put a possum in my makeup bag with my makeup still in it. Besides, Caleb threw the bag away and put Perry in a box until he or she comes out of… Until the possum wakes up."

"Oh. My. Gosh. Grandma, please tell me you didn't take a *dead* possum into the pet shop to have them try to save it!"

Terri was doubled over with laughter. "This is great!"

"Terri, hush," Jade scolded. "It's not great. It's…it's horrible. Grandma, that guy will think you're nuts."

"I'm not nuts, nor does Caleb think I am. The possum was alive when I scooped him up, and Caleb believes Perry is still alive. In fact, he's going to call me when Perry wakes up."

Wiping tears from the corners of her eyes, Terri asked, "Who's going to call you—Caleb or Perry?"

Millie cut Terri a disapproving glance and then addressed Jade. "I'm not as loopy as you two seem to think I am." She looked around the shop until she spotted Mocha. "Aw, there's my boy! He doesn't judge." She went over to pet him. "The young people are having a pre-grand opening mixer in the atrium tonight. You two should go. Maybe gorgeous Caleb will be there."

"He sounds wonderful," Terri said. "This knight in shining—what? Denim, maybe? Saving possums and making women swoon."

Terri lived in one of the apartments upstairs. Jade lived in the house Millie had sold her when she'd moved into her apartment. Millie had chosen the simplicity and socialness of "Community Center life" to continuing to maintain a house.

Since Jade didn't live at the Community Center, she didn't feel comfortable attending the gathering. Besides, she had a sneaking suspicion that her mother was behind Grandma's attempts to cajole her into attending the party and singing the praises of Mr. Pet Shop. Next, she'd be asking Grandma to leave job listings for Jade by the cash register.

Her mother thought she was wasting her time with a knitting shop. "Too much work and not enough profit." In Mom's opinion, Jade either needed to find a more lucrative career or a rich husband. Jade wasn't in the market for either. She was doing fine, thank-you-very-much.

Seeing that Jade didn't seem to plan on responding to Millie, Terri said, "We'll think about it. Thanks for reminding us."

Jade pointed to the flyers she'd printed out yesterday afternoon. "Terri, don't let me forget to put those flyers up in the library, café, and atrium when I take my lunch break. I already have the information on the Community Center app for the YPs, but I'm afraid the seniors won't see it there."

Millie sniffed. "You act as if we old fogies don't even know what an app is."

"Do you use the app, Grandma? Did you see the information about the beginning knitters' class on there?"

"I prefer to get my news the old-fashioned ways—like newspapers, televisions, and community bulletin boards." She stiffened her back and raised her chin. "But I *do* know what an app is and how to use it if I'm so inclined."

"We know, Millie," Terri said. "You're cooler than most of the other seniors around here."

"Yes, well…"

That was Millie's way of shrugging off a compliment.

As her grandmother left, Jade turned to Terri. "Did she *really* just come in here and tell us she rescued a possum that might or might not be living?"

Terri nodded.

She blew out a breath and looked around the shop. The white floor-to-ceiling blocks contained various colors and types of yarn. An oak stepladder on wheels stood waiting by the window for someone to need something from a top shelf. A padded navy bench sat in front of the window and was a wonderful place to knit when things got slow in the shop. Those moments didn't happen often, but Jade appreciated them when they did.

In fact, she wished she could sit down now and process what had happened. She really needed to talk to that pet shop guy and try to explain to him that Grandma wasn't crazy. Sure, she could be a little ditzy now and then—forgetful sometimes—but not crazy. Definitely not crazy. Although putting a possum in a makeup bag was pretty nutso.

Terri interrupted Jade's reverie. "Here they come."

Jade had no idea why children struck such fear in her petite blond friend's heart, but she was having fun playing on that fear this morning. "Wish me luck."

"See you on the other side."

The eight girls came squealing into the shop. Jade introduced herself and had them tell her their names. She repeated them and made it a point to remember them.

"First, let's pick out your yarn."

"Is it all right if I go over and make sure everything is set up for their tea party at the café?" the mom asked, one foot already back out the door.

"That's fine," Jade said. "If I need you, I'll send Terri to get you."

"All righty. If I don't hear from you, I'll be back in an hour." She paused. "Will they be done in an hour? I can give you more time if you need it."

"An hour will be fine," Jade said firmly. "Their scarves won't be finished by then, but they'll be well on their way and the girls

10

will know how to complete them. Should they need any help, they can always come back."

Jade was more frazzled than she'd expected to be when the girls finally galloped off to the café with the birthday girl's mom.

"That was an excellent sale," Terri said.

"I earned every penny of it. From the cast-on row to explaining that fringe was a little too advanced for them on this project." She looked around. "Where's Mocha?"

"He hid when the girls stormed in. I imagine he'll come out soon."

"Hidey-ho!" Greta Parker blasted through the door.

"What I said about Mocha coming out? Scratch that," Terri said under her breath.

Greta was a force of nature. She had short auburn hair with streaks of plum. Today she wore jeans and a baseball shirt bearing the logo for the group Imagine Dragons. Gold sparkly sneakers completed the outfit.

"I like your shirt," Jade said. "Are you a fan?"

"Oh, yes! Imagine if there *were* dragons." Greta put up her hands and spread them out slowly as if to illustrate the magnitude of such an idea. "Like in that show everyone is wild over. I haven't got to see it yet. I'm waiting to have enough time to binge it."

Nope. Just as Jade had suspected, Greta didn't realize Imagine Dragons was a music group. She thought it was a suggestion.

Terri jerked her head in the direction of the knitting room. "Are you gonna work a while? I'll be glad to help you get something from your project locker."

The knitting room contained four vertical cabinets. Each cabinet had four tiered spaces for a total of sixteen cabinets. At present, ten of the doors contained the name of regular patrons. Jade was sure they'd fill up once the shop had been open a bit longer.

"No, thanks, dolls," Greta said. "I'm looking for Millie. Have you seen her?"

"Not since this morning," Jade said. She decided not to tell Greta about the possum incident.

"Oh, well, I'll find her. And if you see her before I do, tell her I'm looking for her."

"Why don't you just call her?" Terri asked.

"I'm almost out of minutes." With that, Greta was gone.

"It's safe to come out now, Mocha," said Terri.

The cat obviously didn't believe her and remained in his hiding place.

"Don't be so hard on Greta," Jade said. "She's…well, she's unique."

"I know. It's just that she and I are the senior and YP liaisons for the grand opening celebration, and I feel like she isn't doing enough for the seniors. She's trying her best to be a millennial, and it ain't happening."

Chapter Two

❀

JADE DECIDED THAT ASKING Caleb at Hightail It! Pet Supply and Grooming for permission to put a flyer for the knitting class in his shop would be a good excuse to talk with him and reassure him that Millie wasn't insane. Well, not completely, anyway. She could still hardly believe her grandmother had taken a *possum*—be it dead or alive—in her makeup bag, no less, to the pet shop. What had she been thinking?

She walked into the shop, self-conscious about the bells over the door drawing attention to her as she stepped across the threshold.

"Hi!" called a handsome man at the register ringing up the purchase of a woman with a Yorkie in her arms. "Be right with you."

He had to be Caleb. There couldn't be two drop-dead gorgeous guys working in this shop, could there? If so, she needed to call Terri and have her friend close up shop and join her. At least Millie hadn't been exaggerating about Caleb's looks.

The woman with the Yorkie finished her transaction, smiled and batted her eyelashes at Caleb a few more times, and then brushed past Jade, leaving a waft of flowery perfume in her wake.

Jade turned to make sure the woman had, indeed, gone before saying to the handsome man at the register, "She smelled good. Or else the dog did."

He laughed. "Well, Princess did have a bath this morning."

She resisted the temptation to ask whether Princess was the dog or her haughty owner. Instead, she said, "My grandmother was in here this morning. She brought you…a possum."

"Millie! Yeah! I was just getting ready to call her."

So, she'd been right in guessing this was Caleb.

"Perry is awake and considering tasting the electrolyte and water solution I offered him—or her." He jerked his head toward the back of the shop. "Wanna see?"

"Um, okay."

Caleb used the microphone next to the register to tell someone named Aidan that he was going into the back for a minute. Then he headed for the back of the shop.

Jade fell into step beside him.

"You *are* a pretty redhead," he said.

"Excuse me?"

He chuckled. "Millie said her granddaughter was a pretty redhead."

She rolled her eyes. "I'm sorry. She can be a bit much sometimes."

"I thought she was a delight. Not that many people would be so kindhearted as to pick up a baby possum in a makeup bag. Most folks would've thought, 'Eh, it's just a possum.' But not Millicent Fairchild."

Jade didn't respond. She was digesting the fact that Caleb had just called her grandmother by her full name.

"And unless I miss my guess," Caleb continued, "that wasn't an inexpensive bag."

"Probably not." She stopped. "Just how long did you and my grandmother talk this morning? I mean, you seem to know an awful lot about her."

"Not really." He shrugged. "I know her name, that she had a nice makeup bag that she emptied in order to save a baby animal, that she lives upstairs, and that she has a pretty, red-haired granddaughter. Oh, and she seems to like alliteration. Is that a lot to know about someone?"

Jade was mortified that her grandmother had spent the morning talking her up to this guy. And then Jade herself had rushed over at the first opportunity. Caleb must think Jade was laughably desperate. "Whatever. Look, I need to get back."

"I thought you wanted to see Perry," he said.

"No, I'm good. You can work all that out with my grandmother. Good luck with the…Perry." She turned and stalked out of the store.

She realized when she returned to Nothin' But Knit that she still had the flyer in her hand. She slammed it onto the counter, causing a customer to turn in surprise.

"Sorry," Jade mumbled. "I didn't mean to startle you. Would you be interested in taking our beginners' knitting class?"

"Honey, I've been knitting the biggest part of my life," the customer retorted.

"Oh. Good. Well, you've come to the right place then." She smiled, feeling like an idiot.

She hated that she'd let her irritation get the best of her at the pet shop, but she couldn't help it. She could just imagine her grandmother in the shop trying to fix her up with Caleb, and it made her blood boil. She expected that sort of behavior from her mother, but how dare Grandma interfere with her personal life? They'd always had each other's backs. Now, it seemed, Grandma had Mom's back. And to think a guy like Caleb would be interested in Jade—and vice versa—was ridiculous.

Fighting tears, she strode over to the window and looked out at the parking lot. There was a maple tree on the grass that bordered the lot, and it was beautiful—large branches, thick with bright green leaves. In a few weeks, those leaves would begin turning yellow and red.

She started when Terri touched her shoulder. "You all right?"

Jade nodded.

"Good. Ms. Easterling is coming down to talk with Greta and me. She wanted to have a quick meeting here."

Sandra Easterling was the forty-something manager of the Kinsey Falls Living and Retail Community Center. Neither a senior nor a young professional, she was theoretically hired for her ability to relate to both groups. Even her apartment, which was adjacent to the Community Center office, was centrally located between the two groups.

"I can handle things in the shop, if you guys would prefer to meet in one of the conversation rooms," Jade said.

"I'll see what Sandra wants to do. I just hope she could track down Greta."

"And that Greta was willing to use the necessary minutes to take the call." Jade gave her friend a slight smile.

"Did you see that guy, Caleb?"

Jade nodded. "Yeah. I doubt I'll ever see him again though. He probably thinks I'm a real snot."

"Why?" Terri asked. "What did you do?"

"I was pretty abrupt with him. He was going to show me the possum, and I was following him into the back. Then he started talking about Grandma, and I said I had to leave."

She narrowed her brown eyes. "Did he say something mean about Millie?"

"No, he was complimentary…even complimented *me* by saying I must be her pretty redhaired granddaughter. But to think Grandma went over there to try to fix me up with him makes me so angry."

Terri huffed. "She didn't go there to fix you up with anyone. She went there to save a baby possum. I think that's kinda sweet, albeit a little icky. I mean, not as icky if it had been a snake. But then I can't see Millie picking up a snake." She inclined her head. "Had you asked me prior to this morning though, I'd have never imagined her picking up a possum."

"The reason she went over there is beside the point," said Jade. "All of a sudden, she's trying to get me a boyfriend. I don't like it. Besides, how pathetic does that make me look? My grandma thinks she needs to help me get a date."

"Well, talk with her about it. When you can do so calmly and rationally. There's Ms. Easterling." Terri hurried over to greet the Community Center's manager.

"Hi, Terri," Sandra said. "I'm sure you're busy today. Thank you for making time for me."

"No problem. Did you get in touch with Greta?"

"She should be here—"

"Hidey-ho!" Greta called as she came into the shop.

There was a flash of brown as Mocha raced to hide in his bed under the counter.

"And there she is now," Sandra said. "Where would it be best to talk?"

"There's no one in the knitting room at the moment." Terri led the women into the knitting room, and they took seats at the table.

Jade wasn't trying to eavesdrop, but she couldn't help but hear the women's conversation. She wondered if she should tell them, but then she decided that since the shop was currently empty and their discussion wasn't likely confidential, she'd let it go.

Sandra was speaking. "So, here's the thing: the grand-opening celebration is in a week, and the two of you can't agree on anything."

"I can't help it if Terri wants to be an old fuddy-duddy."

"Greta, you're only thinking about the young professionals. You're not sparing any thought at all for your people."

"My people? *My* people? I thought the point of all of us living here together was to become a united group. How can we do that if we still have *my* people and *your* people?"

"Ladies," Sandra interrupted sharply. "This has to stop. If you can't pull everything together, compromise, and provide me with the entertainment and food to be served by Monday, then I'll do everything myself. And, sadly, neither of you will get any credit. Nor will you have the opportunity to help coordinate any other Kinsey Falls LRCC events."

"You mean, we won't get our names in the paper?" Greta asked. "But, I've already been looking forward to talking to that reporter, that—what's his name—Mitch Reedy?"

Jade recalled that Mitch Reedy was an attractive field reporter for one of the local television news teams.

"There's nothing I'd like more than to be able to tell Mitch Reedy that you two planned everything and have him do an in-depth interview with each of you," Sandra said. "And if I have the information I need by Monday, that's what we'll do. May I count on you to work out your differences?"

By this time, Sandra was striding out of the knitting room with Terri and Greta trailing in her wake.

"Yes, ma'am," said Terri.

"You can count on *me*," Greta began.

Terri shot her a look of pure venom.

"And Terri," Greta finished lamely. "You can count on me and Terri. We'll figure this out."

"Thank you." Sandra left the two women standing inside Nothin' But Knit glaring at each other.

"So, now what?" Greta asked, as soon as Sandra was out of earshot.

"You and I get together after I get off work and do what you told Sandra we'd do—figure this out."

"Do you need a referee?" Jade asked.

Both Terri and Greta vowed they didn't, but Jade wasn't convinced.

Chapter Three

AFTER MILLIE UNPACKED AND put away her groceries, she hurried downstairs to Hightail It! to see Caleb and Perry. Caleb was with customers—a woman and two children—when she walked in. He grinned and winked at Millie over top of the woman's head.

She smiled. He was beautiful. Jade was beautiful. They could make her some gorgeous great-grandbabies. And Jade could knit up the cutest little booties, hats, and blankets for them.

Caleb brought the woman's purchases up to the counter. It appeared the children would have everything they needed to take care of a puppy. As Caleb scanned the items, the boy and girl yammered to him about their new dog.

"It's a boxer," the boy said.

"Yeah, and Daddy wanted to name her Ali, who was a famous boxer, but our puppy is a *girl!*"

"We went with Allie," the woman said. "Close enough, right?"

"Right. Just as long as Allie can float like a butterfly and sting like a bee," Caleb said.

The boy scrunched up his face. "I think you're confused. Allie is a dog."

When the trio left, Millie chuckled. "Youth is wasted on the young. Who said that?"

"Shaw," Caleb answered.

"That's right—George Bernard Shaw. I'm impressed that you know that."

"He preferred to be called Bernard. Didn't care much for *George*."

"How do you know?" Millie asked.

"He used to come in here, buy things for his boxer."

She laughed. "I was so relieved to get your call about Perry. I really thought I'd killed the little thing—given it a heart attack or something."

"He's just fine. Want to go see?"

"Yes, please."

Millie followed Caleb into the back where little Perry cuddled on a heating pad. There was room inside the box where Perry could crawl away if he got too warm.

"The vet brought that over for us to borrow," Caleb said, nodding toward the heating pad. "And although he said Perry appears to be healthy, our vet can't really help us. He recommended we call a licensed wildlife rehabilitator who would know more about possums."

"Did he recommend someone?"

"Yes. He said there's a wonderful rehab center in Elizabethton. He gave me their number, and I left a message for someone to return my call."

Millie pointed toward a medicine dropper and a small bottle. "What's that? Did he give you some kind of medicine for him?"

"It's actually water mixed with an electrolyte formula. This is what we're supposed to feed Perry, provided we can get him to eat."

"How often do you feed him?"

"I try every hour or so. I've been successful once, but that's it."

"Well, you shouldn't have to do all this on your own," said Millie. "I'm the one who found him. I'll be happy to take him to my apartment and take care of him there."

"Really?" He arched a brow. "You'll be *happy* to do that?"

"Well, I won't be thrilled, but I do feel like Perry is my responsibility. Yet here you are doing all the work."

"I don't mind. I'm actually glad I was able to help keep him alive and to figure out what to do for him. And once we hear from the wildlife refuge, I can take him to Elizabethton."

"Nothing doing. *We'll* take him. I'll drive. You hold Perry."

"Deal." He grinned. "Tell you what—meet me here when I get off work at five this afternoon. We'll check on Perry, grab a bite to eat, and decide then who gets to keep him for the night. Unless the rehab people call and want us to get him there right away."

"All right."

* * *

Jade was tidying up the knitting room when Millie breezed in. She could hear her grandmother talking with Terri.

"Be right there, Grandma," Jade called.

"…cutest little thing!" Millie was gushing when Jade entered the room. "And Caleb has fixed Perry the nicest temporary home. One of the local veterinarians stopped by Hightail It! and loaned—"

"I take it the Knight in Shining Denim has struck again?" Jade asked wryly.

"Indeed, he has," said Millie. "And be as sarcastic as you want, but Caleb is a gem. I think the world of him."

Jade shrugged one shoulder. "He didn't seem that great to me."

Millie frowned. "When did you meet him?"

"I went over there to see that possum." *And to try to convince that guy you aren't out of your mind*, Jade added silently.

"And did you see it? Isn't it adorable?"

"I didn't see it. I had all I could take of Caleb before we got to the back of the store, so I told him I needed to leave," she said. "He didn't tell you I'd been there?"

"Nope. We just talked about Perry and made plans for dinner this evening."

Jade's jaw dropped. "You what?"

"We're going to have dinner later and decide what to do with Perry over the weekend. The shop is closed tomorrow."

Jade blinked.

"Are you kidding me?" Terri asked. "You got a date with this guy? I've *got* to see him now."

"I wouldn't call it a date," Millie said, trying but failing to keep her lips from curving into a smile. "We're simply meeting to discuss what to do with the baby possum until we can take Perry to the wildlife rehab center."

"Wait—until *we* take Perry? Who's we?"

"Caleb and I. Keep up, Jade."

"I have *so* got to see this guy. Hold down the fort, Jade. I'm going to buy Mocha a toy."

"Terri—"

Jade's attempt to keep Terri in Nothin' But Knit fell on deaf ears. She turned back to her grandmother. "You don't even know this guy."

"Sure, I do. We're bonding over a possum."

Greta came by to collect Terri just before Nothin' But Knit closed.

"I've reserved us a spot in the library because I thought we might need a computer."

Terri merely nodded, not mentioning that anything they could look up on the computer Terri could check on her phone. "I'm sure we can work quickly. Do you have any plans for later this evening?"

"Millie and I had talked about getting some food and watching a movie, but she had something come up."

Terri tried unsuccessfully to hide a grin as Jade slammed the cash register drawer closed.

"I guess I *could* go over to the party in the atrium tonight," Greta said. "Are you planning to go?"

"Yes, but it's a young professionals' gathering, Greta. It isn't a...a joint affair like the grand opening celebration."

"I know. But I was invited."

Behind Greta's back, Terri rolled her eyes at Jade. Jade simply shook her head. Why *wouldn't* Greta be invited to the mixer? After all, her grandmother was dining out with the gorgeous pet shop guy right now. Maybe they were living in some sort of parallel universe, and Terri and Jade simply weren't aware of it yet. Maybe handsome old guys would be stopping by Nothin' But Knit any minute to sweep them off their feet.

Terri and Greta headed for the library, and Jade closed up the shop.

Later that evening, Jade was home on the sofa watching *Downton Abbey* while Mocha snoozed on the ottoman. Jade was knitting white bookmarks to be given away at the upcoming grand opening celebration. Once the knitting was complete, she threaded thin ribbon in a contrasting color—purple, pink, blue, red, yellow, or green—throughout the bookmarks to attach a Nothin' But Knit business card to each one.

She'd hoped to have added about ten to her collection tonight, but she was finding it difficult to concentrate on her knitting or the Dowager Countess. All she could think about was Millie. Millie and Caleb.

Their working together to save the life of a wild animal was one thing...she guessed. But wasn't talking about the animal over dinner going a little too far? What could they possibly have to talk about? To Jade, it was simple. Either her grandmother or Caleb would keep the possum and hopefully help it stay alive until one of them—*one* of them—could take it to the wildlife rescue on Monday. That was a five-minute conversation at most.

Something else Jade didn't get was why they *both* needed to transport the possum to Elizabethton. She hadn't gone with Caleb to look at the thing, but just how big could it be? Was it truly large enough to warrant a two-person transport team? Jade didn't think so.

Jade knew nothing about Caleb, and neither did Millie. Sure, Terri came back from the pet shop with a package of foil balls for Mocha and a squealy account of how gorgeous and charming Caleb was. But Jade had plenty of experience with handsome guys—all of it bad.

She remembered when she was in high school with her braces and glasses, how red she'd turn when one of the football players would speak to her. It was a game to them. Who could flirt with skinny, mousy Jade Burt and be the first to make her blush that day? Then they'd all laugh at her mortification while they gave each other high-fives. And that didn't even skim the surface of what Blake had done.

Handsome, charming guys were users. They took what they wanted and didn't care who they hurt. She wondered what Caleb wanted from her grandmother. Was he a con man? Did he prey on lonely older women and take money from them? The thought of Caleb taking advantage of Millie made Jade furious. That man had better think twice before making her grandma a target.

She put aside her knitting and grabbed her purse and car keys. She needed to talk with Terri.

Chapter Four

MILLIE STUDIED CALEB FROM across the dimly-lit steakhouse table. He was eating his third buttered roll. Ah, to have the metabolism of a twenty-something again.

He looked a bit sheepish as he pushed the basket containing the last remaining roll toward her. "You should try these. They're really good."

"I'll take your word for it," she said with a smile.

"I feel like I'm being a pig."

"I'm glad you have a healthy appetite."

"Thanks for suggesting this place," he said. "I like it."

"You've never eaten here before?"

"Once or twice, but I don't make it a habit."

Of course, Millie thought. *Graduate student.* "Well, tonight is my treat."

"Oh, no, ma'am. I wouldn't dream of having you pay for my dinner. That's not why I asked you to eat with me. We're here to discuss Perry."

"And we're here discussing Perry because of me."

"You were kind enough to pick him up and bring him in. Most people would've passed right by," said Caleb.

"I'm certainly not most people."

"Besides, I…" He shrugged. "I don't know. I hate eating alone."

"I know you said there was no Mrs. Caleb. Isn't there a Mrs. Caleb wannabe?"

"Not anymore. I was seeing a girl, but she was… Well, she and I didn't really click. So, we broke up."

"Recently?"

He nodded. "Worst part is she lives at the Community Center."

"Ah. You still have to see her?"

"Not often."

"But it hurts when you do?" Millie asked gently.

"It's not that as much as it's just awkward. I should've used better judgment when it came to dating someone who lived in the same apartment building."

So, would that be a strike against Jade? She didn't live *at the Community Center, but would Caleb distance himself because he didn't want to date someone who worked in the building? Slow down, Millie. You're getting ahead of yourself.*

"What about you?" Caleb asked. "Are you seeing anyone?" At her raised brows, he chuckled. "I didn't mean it that way. I just hope I didn't interrupt any plans you had."

"I was planning to eat dinner in front of the television with a friend. But we can do that anytime. It's not everyday one rescues a possum."

He laughed. "Let's hope not anyway."

She realized she hadn't answered his question, so she said, "I'm *not* seeing anyone. Do you have a rich uncle or someone in mind for me?"

"'Fraid not." He sipped his soda. "And I get the feeling you were trying to fix me up with your granddaughter, but I don't think she's interested."

"Why do you say that?"

"She came in earlier today to talk with me about the baby possum. I asked her if she'd like to see Perry, and she said yes." He flipped his palms. "We were making small talk when she just bolted. I don't know if it was something I said or what."

"Don't think another thing about it," said Millie. "Jade has always been a little backward. It takes her a while to warm up to new people."

Their food arrived then—salmon for Millie and a thick steak for Caleb. The waitress lingered, asking Caleb to cut into his steak to make sure it was satisfactory. Millie noticed how the woman's eyes rested on him. Caleb seemed clueless, but she doubted he was. He had to know how handsome he was.

He asked for a refill on his soda, and the young woman scurried off to get it.

They ate in silence until his soda was delivered. Then he asked her if she was retired.

"I am," said Millie. "I spent thirty years as the office manager for my husband's dental practice."

"That explains your beautiful smile." He raised his glass. "To great teeth."

She laughed. "You are a charmer. I'll give you that." She wondered if he broke off the recent relationship or if the girl did. Either way, she was torn between feeling sad for the end of that romance and hopeful Caleb and Jade would somehow hit it off. "Did you grow up around here?"

"About three hours from here…a little town called Maynardville, Tennessee."

"And how'd you end up in Kinsey Falls?" Millie asked.

"I went to Old Dominion University and got my bachelor's degree in public service. And then I kinda ran out of money, and I didn't want to have student loans hanging over my head half my life."

"I can certainly understand that."

"My college roommate was from Kinsey Falls, and in fact, his dad owns Hightail It!. So, after I graduated, I came here to work—

cheaper cost of living, most everything I need is under one roof—and I take my graduate classes, two at a time, online."

"It sounds like you have an excellent head on your shoulders."

"Thanks," he said with a smile.

"Old Dominion is in Norfolk, isn't it? Do you miss it?"

"I miss the beach and Chesapeake Bay, not that I got to spend all that much time there. But Kinsey Falls is beautiful too. I'm really looking forward to seeing this wildlife rescue center in Elizabethton. I bet there's some great hiking trails nearby."

They finished their meal and walked outside to get into Millie's Mercedes.

"Ms. Fairchild, how many teeth did you have to put under your pillow for the tooth fairy to bring you *that*?" he asked.

"All the baby teeth in Kinsey Falls." She laughed. "Wanna drive us home?"

"Yes, ma'am!"

She tossed him the keys.

* * *

When Terri hadn't answered her phone, Jade guessed her friend had decided to go to the mixer. She arrived at the atrium to the pounding beat of pop music. She looked around nervously at groups of people standing to the side of what had apparently been designated the dance floor. There were some couples—and a few singletons—dancing, but most people were participating in yelled conversations. A refreshment table had been set up near the DJ.

She didn't know any of these people. How would she pick Terri out in this crowd? Terri and Jade had their social awkwardness in common—it's why they'd gravitated to each other during that first horrible year in middle school. Terri might not even be here. She should probably go.

As she turned to leave, she caught sight of the back of an auburn head with plum-colored highlights.

Was that really Greta? Had she actually crashed the YP party?

"Hidey-ho, darlins!"

She had.

Jade cringed for Greta. The woman was about to get told—likely in the nastiest of terms—that she wasn't welcome here.

But the group Greta addressed *was* welcoming her. A handsome young man with sandy hair slung his arm around her shoulders. That's when Jade noticed that Terri was walking behind Greta.

"...the best, Greta. Thanks!"

Jade placed her hand on Terri's arm, causing her friend to start.

"Jade! You decided to come. I'm so glad."

With an incredulous frown, Jade nodded toward Greta, who was addressing the good-looking guy.

"Well, now, Justin, I know you don't particularly care for the gluten free, low-carb fare—lucky you for not having to watch your weight yet. I made you a chocolate chip cake. Half of it is in this cake pan with the brownies, and the other half is at my place waiting for you to come and get it."

"Yes!" He hugged Greta. "Here, I'll put those on the dessert table, and I'll be right back." He took the cake pan and headed toward the refreshments.

"You look pretty," a dark-haired girl with bright blue eyes told Greta.

"Oh, sweetie, thank you. You look gorgeous."

"How are you doing on that hibiscus tea?" the girl asked.

"I'm still good for now. I'll let you know when I need more."

Justin returned as the DJ fired up a slow song. He grabbed Greta's hand. "Dance with me."

"Can you waltz?" Greta asked.

"Heck, yeah. I was top of my class in cotillion." Greta laughed as she allowed the young man to lead her onto the dance floor.

Jade and Terri looked on in astonishment.

"Parallel universe," Jade muttered.

29

"Isn't he a dream?" the dark-haired girl said. "He treats Greta like she's his aunt or something."

When Justin and Greta returned from their dance, Greta was saying she didn't particularly care for that guy's music.

"He never sings anything upbeat and happy." Greta noticed them. "Oh, hi. Terri and Jade, this is Justin and Kelsey. These girls own the knitting shop downstairs."

"Knitting shop?" Justin echoed. "Greta, do you knit?"

"I sure do."

"You're the total package—you bake, you knit. Is there anything you *can't* do?"

Greta grinned all over her happy little face. "Not much, darlin'. I'll make you a pretty scarf come winter—you too, Kelsey. You'll just have to let me know what colors you'd like."

Terri said, "If you'll excuse me, I'm going to get a bottle of water."

"Me too." Jade fell into step beside Terri. "Are you having fun?"

"No."

As soon as they were far enough away from Greta and her millennial friends, Jade asked, "Then can we please get out of here?"

"Not fast enough," said Terri. "I think we're in an episode of the freakin' *Twilight Zone.*"

Terri unlocked her door and turned on the lights. Jade was still surprised that all the apartments—despite having the exact same floorplan and much of the same furniture—could look so different. Each apartment was furnished with a brown leather sofa, chair, and ottoman in the living room, a maple four-chair table in the kitchen, and a double bed with drawers underneath it for storage. Millie had decorated hers to be classy and minimalist. Terri's was modern and shabby chic. And Greta's place was bold and bright.

"Want a drink?" Terri asked.

"I could go for a bottle of water." She sank onto the sofa.

Terri brought them each a bottle of water and sat down beside Jade. "I was so uncomfortable and claustrophobic in that crowd. And, yet, Greta breezed in there like she'd known those people all her life."

"Grandma has that easy way about her too. I mean, this morning, she found a baby possum, and this evening she's on a date with her fellow rescuer."

"Are you worried it's an actual date?"

"No. Not really. I mean—" She sighed. "I don't want Grandma to fall for some sweet-talking con man."

"Millie is smarter than that."

"You'd think. But smart, lonely women get taken in by scammers all the time."

"Still, Jade, this guy didn't seek Millie out. He didn't target her like some random stalker or something."

"I know. I'm probably just overreacting." She sighed. "Did you and Greta make any progress on the party planning?"

"We did, actually. I asked Greta what types of things the seniors would enjoy. She got a little huffy and said there were a ton of things both groups would enjoy."

"Like what? Making brownies for the YPs?" She shook her head. "Sorry. I'm just in a bad mood. So, what did you come up with?"

"Bingo."

"Bingo?" Jade echoed. "Well, that is good for the golden oldies."

"Well, that's what I thought, but when Greta started talking about it, I realized it could be good for everybody."

Jade started humming the theme from the *Twilight Zone*.

"I'm serious," Terri said. "Greta suggested getting Community Center vendors to donate prizes."

"That does sound like a good idea."

"And we even thought we might get Sandra to spring for a small cash prize out of the celebration budget."

"Good luck with that."

"Even if she doesn't, I'm sure the vendors will pony up some terrific prizes. Don't you think?"

"Yeah," said Jade. "Yeah, I do."

Not wanting her cynical attitude to diminish Terri's excitement, Jade said she was tired and that she needed to get back home.

Chapter Five

❀

THE NEXT MORNING, JADE got ready early, fed Mocha, and headed for the Kinsey Falls Living and Retail Community Center. She went to the café and bought coffee and pastries before heading up to her grandmother's apartment.

Millie answered the door in her robe and slippers. "Jade! What a nice surprise. I wasn't expecting you today."

"I brought coffee and pastries. I thought we might have a girls' day."

"That sounds fantastic. Let me run and slip my clothes on."

"Is the baby possum here?" Jade asked.

"Not yet. Perry stayed with Caleb last night, but I'm supposed to keep him tonight. Caleb is bringing him over to me this afternoon."

Jade waited in the kitchen while Millie got dressed. She busied herself putting the pastries on a platter and getting each of them a dessert plate.

"If you're here long enough, you can meet them both," Millie said, entering the kitchen in jeans and a thin, short-sleeved white sweater. "Oh, wait, you've already met Caleb, haven't you? He doesn't think you like him very much, but I told him that it sometimes takes you a while to warm up to folks."

"Gee, thanks for talking about me to a stranger, Grandma."

"He's not a stranger. At least, not to me. We're friends." She plucked a bear claw from the platter and placed it on her dessert plate. "Have you spoken with your mom this week?"

"No. I've been busy."

"Uh-huh. You've been busy, or you simply didn't want to talk with her?"

Jade raised her chin. "Both."

Her relationship with her mother had always been strained. Jade had never felt that she'd lived up to Fiona's high standards, and Fiona had never done anything to alleviate her daughter's insecurities. The tension between them had worsened when Jade had announced her plan to open a knitting shop with Terri. Fiona thought the idea was frivolous and that Jade would be declaring bankruptcy within a year. Then her mother had fallen back on her old standby, "You need to find a decent job, at least until you can land a man financially equipped to take care of you." Jade thoroughly resented the fact that Fiona believed her to be too ignorant to make her own career decisions—or relationship decisions, for that matter—or to even take care of herself financially.

"She's not supposed to be dropping in anytime today, is she?" Jade asked.

"No. You're safe." Millie grinned. "You should know I wouldn't dream of inviting Fiona over knowing I might have a possum in the house. Can you imagine the conniption your mother would have over that?"

They both laughed.

"Don't shut her out of your life, Jade," Millie said softly. "She loves you and only wants what's best for you."

"She wants me to have what's best for *her*. The things that make her happy aren't the things that make me happy, Grandma. If Mom had her way about it, I'd either be a doctor or married to a doctor and be a stay-at-home mom to half a dozen kids."

"Your mother wants you to feel secure. She never had any security. After your father left, she struggled to raise you on her own until she married your stepdad and could do a better job providing for you." Millie shook her head. "Your granddad and I helped where we could, but Fiona was too proud to let us help much. Most of what we did, we had to do behind her back."

"I know all that. But things are different for me—I'm not married, I don't have a child, I'm not tied down."

"Still, try to look at the situation through a different lens. You're looking through the lens of a daughter being harangued by an overprotective mother. Try the lens of a mother who's terrified that her daughter will suffer any sort of harm."

There was a knock at the door. Jade was glad for the reprieve. While she appreciated her grandmother's suggestion to look at the situation from both sides, she had to wonder if Millie was doing that. Grandma had always considered Jade's point of view in the past, but she was a tiny bit concerned that her ally might be going over to the dark side. And over there in Fiona-land, there was only one perspective.

When Millie answered the door, Caleb hurried in with Perry in the box.

"I just got a call from the rehab center. They'd had a family emergency and couldn't call me back last night. They want us to bring Perry to them as soon as possible."

"I'll get my purse," Millie said.

"Mind if I tag along?" Jade asked.

"Not a bit," said Caleb.

* * *

At first, it was a fairly quiet trip to Elizabethton. Millie was driving, Jade sat on the passenger side, and Caleb and Perry were in the back.

Millie frowned as the map on her phone had her turn onto yet another narrow, half-hidden road. "This isn't the way I'd normally

35

go to Elizabethton, Jade. Are you sure you put the right address into my phone?"

"I'm positive. The navigator said this was the quickest route. The other way would have taken us fourteen minutes longer," she said. "And I know the idea is to get Perry to the rehabilitators as soon as possible." And her out of this car with Prince Charming and the footman some fairy godmother had turned into a possum.

"Of course, it is." Then Millie saw the sign, and everything made sense. *Welcome to Cherokee National Forest.* The roads would just get curvier and steeper from here on out.

Minutes later, Jade exclaimed, "Grandma, please, slow down!"

"I'm going twenty-five," said Millie. "You said yourself we need to get Perry to the sanctuary on the double."

"But this road is so narrow, and have you *seen* the drop-off on my side of the road?" She held to her seat for all she was worth, and her feet slammed invisible brakes.

"I see it, Jade." Millie didn't need Jade's dramatics while she was winding her car around the curves. She was well aware of the drop-off on Jade's side and the mountain of rock on hers.

"Perry says, 'Whee!'" Caleb said.

Millie laughed, and Jade scoffed.

Millie decided to go along with Caleb's attempt to ease the tension. She pointed out the window when there was a clearing. The sun shone on a town many miles away. "Hey, wonder if that's Jerusalem?"

"What?" Caleb asked with a laugh.

"You know, when Jesus was tempted in the desert, Satan took him up on a high mountain and showed him Jerusalem. That's what that sunny little town over there made me think of."

Caleb chuckled. "Millie, you're a treasure."

"You're nuts," Jade muttered under her breath. "Both of you."

Millie ignored her. *Choose your battles.*

At long last, the road began to straighten out. They missed their next turn, and Millie pulled into a driveway. An older man and woman were sitting on the porch. Both leaned forward in their rockers, squinting to see who was paying them a visit. Millie smiled, waved, and backed out onto the highway. They looked confused, but the homeowners waved back.

"Grandma, you're going to get us shot," said Jade.

"No, I'm not. They were friendly."

She drove slowly to a one-lane road beside a charming white church. There were several cars in the parking lot, and Millie fought the urge to roll down the window to see if she could hear them singing. She loved gospel music.

Within a few hundred feet, the pavement turned to gravel, and she saw the first sign for Wynn Wood Wildlife Sanctuary and Rehabilitation Center. At the top of the hill, Millie stopped the car outside the center's office. A man and woman came out of the building to the right of the office as Millie, Jade, and Caleb got out of the car.

"Caleb Young?" the woman asked.

"Yes. You must be Geri."

Geri nodded. "This is my husband Keith." She stepped over to look inside the box Caleb was holding. "Let's get this little guy inside."

They followed Geri into the office. Then, seeing that the small office would be too cramped with all six of them inside, Keith told Geri to holler if she needed him.

"Okay," she said. "I think we're good."

Caleb placed the box on the chrome-and-wood veneer desk while Millie looked around the room. Decorative plates with painted wolves adorned the walls, as did certifications and wildlife notices. A corkboard contained photographs of baby squirrels, possums, and bunnies, as well as fully grown owls, hawks, and deer. There were also cards warning well-meaning people against behaviors that would harm wildlife, such as feeding bread to ducks.

"Really?" Millie said aloud. "It's bad to feed bread to ducks?"

"It is," Geri said, not glancing up from her examination of the tiny critter in the box. "It's better to give them cracked corn or seeds, if you want to give them something. Those, at least, have nutritional value for them. We've seen too many ducks and geese starve while full of bread. It's best to let them find food on their own."

Millie nearly winced at the guilt she felt when she remembered how often she'd taken Fiona and later Jade to feed the ducks at Sugar Hollow park in Bristol.

"Do you think he'll be all right?" Caleb asked.

"I think so."

"How will you feed him?" he asked. "The poor thing has only had a little bit of the water and electrolyte formula mix the veterinarian recommended."

"I'll tube feed him until he's old enough to eat on his own." She nodded to the clipboard on the counter by Millie. "One of you needs to fill out an intake form."

"I can do it," Caleb said.

Millie moved aside so Caleb could grab a pen and quickly fill out the paperwork as he stood at the counter.

Jade had been studying the corkboard. "I hope you get a good grant from the government for the work you're doing."

"We don't get anything from the state or federal government. We survive on donations from volunteers." Geri picked up the box. "Is there anything else you need before I feed this guy?"

"No," said Caleb.

"Yes," Millie and Jade said in unison.

"I'd like to know another way to get back to Kinsey Falls rather than over that mountain," said Jade.

Geri smiled for the first time since they arrived and instructed them to an alternate route.

"And I'd like to know if we can call and check on Perry—the possum," said Millie.

"We're extremely busy this time of year," Geri began. At the crestfallen look on Millie's face, she added, "But a brief weekly call would be fine."

"Thank you."

* * *

After leaving the wildlife refuge, they started looking for a place to eat. Jade wasn't all that hungry, but it seemed that Millie and Caleb were. That, or her grandmother was intent on feeding Caleb every chance she got.

They found a restaurant offering "Southern-style favorites." As soon as they were seated, Millie announced that she was off to the ladies' room to wash her hands.

"I'll go with you," said Jade.

"If the waitress comes by, I'll have a diet soda please, Caleb," said Millie.

"You got it. Jade?"

"Sweet tea please."

In the bathroom, Jade expected Millie to say something about how handsome or kind Caleb was, but she didn't. Instead, Millie talked about the amazing work being done at the wildlife sanctuary.

"I don't know how they do it," she said. "There are some of those creatures I'd be scared to death of, especially if they were hurt. Not the babies, but the full-grown hawks and owls."

"I didn't even know the place existed. Did you?"

"Not until Caleb said the veterinarian told him to contact the Wynns about Perry." Millie took a lipstick from her purse and touched up her lips. She then turned to Jade. "Ready?"

Jade nodded and held the door for her grandmother. Some days, Jade looked at Millie and thought about how old and frail she looked compared to the grandma she'd grown up with. Younger Millie had been so dynamic. Jade was seeing that grandma again today. Maybe it had been good for her to find an orphaned baby possum…as long as it didn't come with a snake in the grass. Jade was still keeping her eye on Prince Charming.

The women returned to the table to see that their drinks were waiting for them.

Caleb smiled and stood. "My turn."

He came back just as the waitress returned to take their orders. They each told her what they wanted, she said she'd get the orders to the kitchen right away, and then she winked at Caleb.

"The effect you have on waitresses." Millie chuckled after the waitress had gone.

"Hey, I can't help it if they take one look at me and can tell I'm a grad student who works at a prestigious pet boutique. They probably think I come from old money and am an excellent tipper."

"And do you?" Jade asked. "Come from old money?"

"Not really. I just dress like I do. Take today's ensemble, for example. These jeans came from old money—money I had in 2007."

Jade laughed. "You've had them that long?"

"Yep. Care to see the receipt?"

"I'll take your word for it," she said.

"I believe it," said Millie. "I have clothes older than either one of you."

"That's because your style is timeless," said Caleb.

"Flatterer." Millie grinned.

"I mean it," he said. "You give off a classy, elegant vibe."

"And what sort of vibe do *I* give off?" Jade asked.

"Skittish as a wild colt."

Terri had been watching a romantic comedy when Jade knocked on her door.

"Want me to restart this movie?" Terri asked. "It's only been on for about fifteen minutes, and it's funny. And you really look like you could use a laugh."

"No, that's okay," said Jade. "I just… I'm sorry to barge in on you like this."

"You're my best friend. Best friends don't barge." She turned the TV off and patted the couch. "Sit down. You're making *me* nervous."

Jade sat beside Terri and leaned her head back against the sofa cushions. "I don't get this…this friendship between Grandma and Caleb. I mean, yes, I get the whole *we saved a baby possum* thing, but they're like besties now. I'm afraid he's trying to take advantage of her."

"I don't know, but Millie isn't the only golden oldie to make friends with a hot YP, remember. And Greta told me this morning that she's teaching Justin to cook. She even bought him a small slow cooker."

"So, do you think this Justin guy is taking advantage of Greta?"

"If he's taking advantage, she's fully aware of it and is letting him do it. She said they met in the library where he was looking up recipes on the computer. He told her he needed to learn how to cook because it was expensive to eat out and he got tired of eating sandwiches all the time."

"What's it with these golden oldies feeding these young guys? Today after we dropped the possum off at the rehab facility, Grandma bought us lunch. Granted, I offered to pay for mine and Caleb offered to pay for his, but she wouldn't let us. I'm guessing she didn't let him pay for his dinner last night either."

Terri thought about this for a second. "I believe it makes them feel needed."

"But Grandma *is* needed. I need her, Mom needs her—"

"No, you don't. You want her around, but you don't *need* her."

"Well, Caleb doesn't *need* her either," Jade said. "Whose side are you on?"

"I don't think there *is* a side. Maybe Caleb—and Justin too, for that matter—see people as people and don't discriminate because of their age."

"And I do?" Jade got to her feet. "Is that what you're saying?"

"Jade, why are you being so defensive? I'm just trying to see these situations from everyone's point of view, giving everyone the benefit of doubt."

Jade shook her head. "What's gotten into you?"

Terri looked down at the carpet. "I don't know. Greta said she'd help me get to know Justin, Kelsey, and some of the other YPs. I'd really like that. Wouldn't you?"

"Not especially. Work keeps me too busy to socialize."

"C'mon, you haven't had a boyfriend in ages. Get to know this guy, Caleb. He's gorgeous, and he seems like a great person. Give him a chance."

"I've known too many guys who *seem* great but aren't. I know Caleb's type. A woman like me has nothing to offer him. And vice versa."

Terri stood and gently put her hands on her friend's shoulders. "Caleb isn't Blake."

"I don't want to talk about it. I need to get back home and make bookmarks."

Terri's words echoed in Jade's head as she drove home.

Caleb isn't Blake.

Caleb isn't Blake.

Blake.

Blake.

Blake.

The star running back of her high school's football team. Broadshouldered, trim-waisted, tight butt, dark hair that was just a little too long and shaggy, blue eyes that seemed to see into a girl's soul. Every girl in that school—from freshman to senior—had crushed on Blake.

About a week before the homecoming dance, he started talking with Jade. At first, it was just a "hey" or "hi" as they passed each other in the hall. Still, any attention from someone like Blake made Jade blush from her toes to the top of her head.

One day, he asked her how she did on a quiz in a class they shared. She said fine, ducked her head, and was going to walk away when he caught her arm.

"Do you have time to talk? Just for a minute?"

She nodded, feeling her face burn hotter and hotter.

He chuckled. "You know, I think it's cute the way you blush like that."

"Y-you…do?"

"I do. So, why don't you ever talk to me in class?"

She shrugged.

"Oh, I see. Goodie good, afraid of getting in trouble. Is that it?"

"S-something like that."

"Are you planning on coming to the football game Friday night?"

"I don't know," she said.

"I'd like for you to."

She struggled to hide a smile and looked down at her feet.

He leaned in, kissed her cheek, and walked away.

Jade was done for. Her crush blossomed into full-blown teen-angst *I love him with all my heart!* right there in the hallway between her locker and the girls' bathroom.

The next day, Blake passed her a note in class asking her to the homecoming dance. She wrote *yes* on the note and passed it back.

She didn't see Blake the rest of that day, but it didn't matter. They were going to the homecoming dance! She—Jade Burt—was going to the homecoming dance on the arm of the handsomest guy in school! She could hardly wait to get home and tell her mom.

Fiona, of course, was over the moon. At last, Jade was going on a date. Terri was happy too, though she admitted to being a little jealous that it was Jade and not her. As if. Terri was going to the dance with a boy who was in the band, and he was super cute.

Terri came over that day after school and brought her teen magazines. She, Fiona, and Jade had talked about dresses, makeup, and hairstyles the rest of the afternoon.

Jade had been so excited she could barely sleep that night. She hopped out of bed the next morning, eager to make herself look her best before heading to school to see Blake.

She saw him first thing. He was standing there in the hall surrounded by his friends. They all faded away for her—all she saw was Blake...gorgeous Blake...sweet, *he kissed my cheek* Blake...her date for the dance Blake.

Jade strode right up, thinking that as Blake's date, she had every right to step into the circle among his friends.

"Hey, Jade," said Trey, the quarterback. "Are you looking forward to the dance?"

"I am." She didn't even try to hide her broad smile. "Where should we meet after the game, Blake?"

That's when the other guys began to laugh, and Jade's back stiffened as an icy chill snaked through her body.

The guys began handing folded bills to Blake.

"Way to go, bud," said Trey. "I didn't know you had it in you."

Jade stood rooted to the floor, staring at Blake. He wouldn't meet her eyes. "What's going on?"

"Blake won the bet." Trey clapped his running back on the shoulder. "We bet him he couldn't agree to get jittery Jade to say she'd go to the dance with him, but he actually pulled it off."

"Is that true, Blake?" Jade asked. "Was this whole thing a joke?"

"I mean...I'll take you," he said. "I keep my word."

"Don't bother." She turned and walked away amid the laughter of the football players. She didn't think Blake was laughing, but she wasn't about to look back to make sure. When Jade ducked into the girls' bathroom, Terri followed her. She'd been standing behind Jade the whole time.

44

"I wanted to say something mean to them," Terri said. "But it was probably pointless and would just give them some perverse satisfaction. Besides, I needed to see if you're okay."

Jade shook her head. "I'm not…okay." She began to sob.

After a cathartic cry, she washed her face and went to her first period class. During that forty-five-minute period, Jade endured all the whispers and giggles she could stand for the day. She went to the nurse saying she had a stomachache and called Fiona to come and get her. She didn't return to school until Monday. By then, she and Blake were old news because one of the teachers got caught smoking pot with some students in a car in the parking lot. But while Mr. Silcox lost his job and became the object of Monday's whispers and giggles, Jade never quite got over her heartbreak, humiliation, and the distrust the experience left her with.

Chapter Six

T ERRI WAS ALREADY TALKING as she pushed open the door to
Nothin' But Knit on Monday morning. "What should we
donate as a prize for the grand opening celebration? You
know, it's only five days away. We need to offer something good,
something to really get our shop on people's minds, make them want
to come visit."

Jade raised one hand to her temple. "Terri. It's not even nine-
thirty, and you sound buzzed. Have you been drinking?"

"Only coffee. I walked around the building with Greta at eight,
and she told me the café is being super generous. Get this: they're
offering one winner a giant punch card allowing the person to get one
cup of coffee and one pastry free of charge once a week for a year.
Isn't that fantastic?"

"Yeah. Sounds nice."

"But that's not all. They're also providing a gift basket with some
freshly baked goodies." Terri licked her lips. "I'd be thrilled to win
either prize."

"Wait," said Jade. "You're actually planning on playing bingo at
the grand opening celebration?"

"Of course! And you will too once you see some of the prizes
you could win. Justin and his group are in."

Jade closed her eyes. "Are you for real right now? How have you gone from wallflower to budding rose overnight? Or wait—maybe you woke up thirty years older."

"Ha ha. I'm putting myself out there, and I like it. You could be a budding flower if you weren't such a stick in the mud. Now, back to our prize. What do you say to a gift basket filled with yarn, knitting needles, maybe a small loom, and a certificate entitling the winner to a free beginners' knitting class?"

"That sounds like kind of a lot."

"Jade, we're going to look stingy if we don't do something as nice as the other shops. Plus, it'll be a tax write-off."

"What if the person who wins the prize is an avid knitter?"

"Then she—or he—can gift the course to someone else...a daughter or granddaughter, maybe."

Jade still hesitated.

"Look, if you don't want to participate, I'll buy the stuff from our store myself and put the basket together."

"No, I was just thinking. Geez! Some of us obviously haven't had anywhere near the amount of caffeine you've had this morning," said Jade. "Of course, Nothin' But Knit will offer a wonderful gift basket. We'll put it together later today, all right?"

"Great. I have to run and tell Greta to add it to the list of prizes we're presenting to Sandra. Be back soon."

Mocha wound around Jade's ankles. She picked up the cat, nuzzled his fur, and asked, "Do you think I'm a stick in the mud?"

He gave a shortened *meow* that Jade could've sworn sounded like, "Yeah."

* * *

Millie was having a leisurely brunch while watching a documentary about Queen Victoria when Greta arrived.

"Ooh, I love Queen Victoria," said Greta. "She's pretty as a little doll, and did you know she's dating Albert in real life? I think that's the most romantic thing. Don't you?"

"I do." Millie decided not to tell Greta the show she was watching wasn't the BBC drama. She turned off the television. "So, how's the party planning going?"

"It's much better. Terri even walked with me this morning, so we could talk some more. We met Kelsey while we were walking. She looked cute as could be—she was wearing those tight-as-hide britches the young people exercise in and a sports bra, and she was carrying little hand weights. She didn't have time to stop and talk with us, but she waved. And Terri gave her an enthusiastic wave back. I believe that one's starting to come out of her shell a tad."

"I'm glad. I wish Jade would. She's so far back in her shell, we're gonna have to stick a cattle prod in there to make her come out."

"She and Caleb didn't hit it off?" Greta asked.

"They started to. At dinner last night, I saw some real progress. But by the time we got back here, Jade had closed herself off from him again." She shook her head. "The boy is going to give up on her, and I don't blame him."

"What's the matter with her anyway? I've seen that Caleb. He's a handsome boy...well built, doesn't appear to be afraid of hard work. Why wouldn't she like him?"

Millie shrugged. "I believe some boy broke her heart back in high school or something."

"Oh, fiddlesticks. That was ages ago. She needs to let past hurts go and—"

"And go looking for new hurts?" Millie asked, with a grin.

"Well...yeah. She might never skin her knee or break a nail if she stays in that shell all the time, but she'll never really live either."

Millie nodded her agreement. Greta was an expert in living. She hadn't always been. Greta and Millie had been friends ever since Greta and her husband Ray had moved into Millie's neighborhood a

48

decade ago. Then Ray had died just over a year ago, and Greta had seemed determined to spend as much of the rest of her life as possible in that two-bedroom ranch home.

When she'd visit Greta, Millie could see how apathetic and depressed her friend had become. One day she'd said, "Hey, will you do me a favor and go with me to see these micro-apartments at that new retail and residential center?"

Greta had agreed to go…for Millie.

Millie's only intention had been to get Greta out of the house for the day, but she'd fallen in love with the micro-apartments and with the whole idea of the Kinsey Falls Living and Retail Community Center. And Greta had too. They made their plans to get side-by-side apartments.

Having something to look forward to reenergized Greta. One of the first things she did was go to the salon and have her long dull gray hair transformed into the auburn, purple-highlighted bob she now sported. She took carloads of…stuff…to the charitable donation box or to the garbage dump.

At first, Millie was afraid her friend was having some sort of breakdown, but then she realized it was a break*through*. Greta had lost her only child in an accident more than twenty years ago. And even though Ray had been a good husband, he could be controlling at times. He was the one who'd never wanted her to change her hairstyle. He was the one who'd never wanted to get rid of anything. Greta saw her opportunity to wipe the slate clean, and she took it. Millie admired her for that.

Millie and her husband Frank had lived in a slightly larger home, but they'd lived well within their means. Rather than spending money on a larger home and the fanciest furnishings, Frank took two weeks off in the early fall each year, and the couple traveled. Millie couldn't think of anywhere she'd wanted to go that she'd never been.

Frank had been gone for five years. It had been sudden—a massive heart attack while he was playing racquetball. It's how he would've wanted to go, she guessed. But losing him was the hardest thing she'd ever been through, and she couldn't imagine ever taking another trip anywhere without him.

As much as Millie would like to give herself credit for helping Greta find a renewed interest in life after Ray had died, she had to admit that it had been Greta who'd helped her through those darkest days. Fiona and Jade had their own grief to deal with, and Millie had always put on a brave face when they were around. It was Greta who dropped in to make sure Millie was eating, who made Millie laugh with fond remembrances of events the two couples had enjoyed together, and who held Millie's hand and wept with her.

Friends like Greta were harder to find that a diamond ring in a gumball machine. Millie believed Jade and Terri had that kind of friendship. At least, she hoped they did. She wanted Jade to have a good friend to grow old with. Of course, she wanted Jade to have a wonderful man to grow old with too. And right now, she couldn't think of a better candidate for the job than Caleb Young.

* * *

Jade had just rung up a customer's purchase that afternoon when she spotted Caleb going upstairs with a small wrapped gift. She accepted payment, trying to concentrate on counting out the money while watching to see where Caleb was going. Luckily, the woman had given her exact change.

"Thank you so much. Have a great day!" Jade said. "Terri, I'll be right back."

She sprinted out the door and up the stairs. She was winded when she reached the top. Caleb was almost to Millie's door.

"Hey!" she called. "What're you doing?"

"I'm going to see your grandmother. What are you doing—stair sprints?"

"Something like that."

He raised his brows and nodded. "Something like that, huh? I'm guessing you saw me and raced up here because you don't trust me and because you correctly assumed I was going to see Millie."

"What's in the box?"

"An engagement ring." He resumed walked toward Millie's apartment.

"It is not!" She had to take double steps to keep up with his long strides.

"Yep. I'm going to be your step-granddad."

"You are not!"

He merely shrugged and kept walking.

Jade latched onto his arm. "Tell me the truth."

He turned, looked down at her, smirked, and said, "No."

"You're infuriating!"

"I'll make you a deal. If you'll go to dinner with me this evening, I'll tell you what's in the box."

She pressed her lips together. "You wouldn't be asking me to dinner if you were getting engaged to my grandmother, so..." She tried to mimic his smirk. "No."

"Maybe I'm simply hedging my bets. If one beautiful woman tells me no, another might say yes."

Jade stared at him. There was a hint of a smile playing around his mouth. She *knew* he wasn't going to propose to her grandmother. But what if he was playing with Millie's heart? Taking advantage of her generosity?

He shrugged and walked away.

A brunette with bouncy chestnut-colored curls and bouncy everything else sashayed down the hallway in a sports bra and yoga pants. Jade recognized her as the girl who thought Justin was so sweet for being kind to Greta.

"Hi, Caleb." The brunette's voice sounded almost like a purr.

"Hi, Kelsey. What're you doing on this side of the hall?"

"I took Greta some hibiscus tea before my next yoga class." She ran a well-manicured pink nail over the hand in which Caleb held the gift box. "And what are *you* doing on this side of the hall?"

"Delivering a package."

Kelsey wet her lips. "Aren't you sweet?"

"As chocolate."

Jade was sick of the smoldering. "Excuse us. We were having a discussion."

"Oops, sorry. Didn't mean to step on any toes," said Kelsey.

"Never," said Caleb, with a wink.

She smiled. "Hope to see you later. You really should take one of my classes, Caleb. You'd like it."

As Kelsey walked away, Caleb said to Jade, "I thought our discussion was over. I asked you out, and you turned me down. What's left to discuss?"

"Fine. I'll go out with you."

"Don't do me any favors," he said.

Her mind immediately flashed back to standing in that high school hallway. "I'm…I'm sorry. If you've withdrawn the invitation, then I understand."

"Are you sure?"

"Of course. I was rude, and I apologize."

"No, that's not what I'm asking," Caleb said. "Are you sure you'd like to go out with me? Or were you just reacting to—" He grinned.

Jade could feel her face flush as she anticipated his next words. *Kelsey flirting with me.*

"—to really wanting to know what's in this box?"

A relieved laugh bubbled up out of her throat. "I'm sure I'd like to go out with you, *and* I'd really like to know what's in that box."

"Then come with me." He held out his free hand, and Jade hesitated only a second before slipping hers into it.

They walked to Millie's door, and Caleb rang the doorbell.

52

"Excuse me," he said to Jade, before letting go of her hand and dropping to one knee. "Presentation is part of the gift."

When Millie opened the door, Caleb raised the package up over his head. "Madam, I present you with this humble token of my admiration."

Millie laughed and clapped. "Oh, my goodness! I should be recording this moment for posterity!"

"I am," said Jade.

Both Millie and Caleb seemed surprised to see her recording them on her phone.

"Oh, Jade, cut that thing off. I was only kidding! And, Caleb, get up and get in here before you raise a ruckus."

"I love raising ruckuses," he said. "Ruckuses are the easiest things to raise. You never have to feed or groom them, you—"

Millie grabbed his arm and yanked him inside. Jade laughed and put the phone back into her pocket as she followed.

"I can hardly wait to see what that is," Jade said, nodding toward the box.

"Nothing doing," said Millie. "This is my present."

"Sorry. I did kinda tell her she could find out what's in the box."

"Then I'll call you and tell you all about it later," Millie teased Jade.

"Grandma!"

"Fine. Get in here and sit down." Millie led the way into the kitchen. "May I get either of you something to drink?"

"No. I have to get back to work," said Jade. She pointedly looked at Millie's clock.

"I only had to work half a day," said Caleb.

Jade pierced him with a look.

"Would you please open the gift?" he asked.

"Yes," said Millie. "I'll open it before my granddaughter has a conniption."

"Conniptions aren't as nice as ruckuses. Much harder to deal with." His attempt to look innocent made Jade roll her eyes.

"So very true." Millie slowly undid the paper. Then she lifted the lid, squealed with delight, and lifted a furry stuffed animal out of the box. "It's Perry!" She laughed and hugged the creature to her. "Oh, Caleb, thank you! I love it!"

"You're welcome."

"It *is* pretty cute," said Jade. She kissed Millie's cheek. "I really do need to get back. Terri will think I've deserted her."

"I'll pick you up at the store at five-thirty," said Caleb.

She nodded, ducked her head, and hurried out of the apartment.

What in the world had she just agreed to—and why? Had she merely reacted to Kelsey's flirting and taken Caleb up on his offer before he decided he'd prefer to go out with the yoga teacher? Jade had raced up those stairs because she hadn't trusted Caleb not to be trying to take advantage of her grandmother. That hadn't changed simply because he'd taken her hand and asked her to dinner, had it? She *had* to be stronger than that, or else she and Millie were both in danger of being taken in by a handsome face and a little flattery.

By the time Jade made it back downstairs, she'd convinced herself that she was going out with Caleb to see what she could learn about him. If he was a smooth-talking grifter, surely Jade would know it before the night was over. Right?

Chapter Seven

"LET ME GET YOU a cup of coffee," Millie said to Caleb, who sat at her kitchen table trying to look innocent.

"I'd rather have water. Straight from the tap is fine."

She got him a bottle of water from the fridge and sat down across from him. "Want to tell me what that was about?"

"What *what* was about?"

"Your telling Jade that you'd pick her up at five-thirty."

"Oh, *that*. Yeah."

She picked up the plush possum. "I'm going to beat you to death with this, if you don't fess up right now."

He laughed. "Jade saw me bringing you a wrapped package, and she wanted to know what was in it. I told her it was an engagement ring and that I was going to be her step-granddad."

Millie placed the possum on her left hand. "It's a tad ostentatious, but all right. Go on."

"She said it was too big to be an engagement ring and insisted on knowing what was in the box. I told her I'd let her see it if she agreed to go out with me tonight."

"I thought you told me you didn't want to date anyone else who lived in the Community Center."

"I did tell you that," he said. "But Jade doesn't live here."

"No, but she works here. Right next door to your shop, as a matter of fact."

He held up an index finger. "One, it's not *my* shop." He added the middle finger. "Two, it's only one date. We might not even hit it off."

"Maybe not, but I worry that one or both of you will end up getting hurt."

Caleb lowered his hand. "I'm tough as nails." When Millie continued to look concerned, he said, "I thought you were lobbying for this."

"I was—*am*."

"Why are you having second thoughts?" he asked. "You think I'd intentionally hurt your granddaughter?"

"No."

"Do you think she'd intentionally hurt me?"

"No. But Jade has a tendency to push people away."

"Like I said, it's one date. We might not even hit it off."

Who wouldn't hit it off with you? Millie kept the thought to herself.

* * *

Jade was breathless and flushed when she returned to Nothin' But Knit.

"What's going on?" Terri asked.

"Nothing. I just went to check on Grandma, that's all."

"Is she all right?"

Jade nodded. "She's fine."

Terri moved to stand in front of her, hands on hips, eyes narrowed. "What are you not telling me?"

With a shrug, Jade admitted, "I ran into Caleb. He asked me out for this evening. And I agreed to go."

Terri gave a whoop and hugged Jade. "It's about time you crawled out of the shell you've been hiding in!"

56

"Let's not get carried away. It's one date, if he even shows up."

"Oh, he'll show up. What are you wearing?"

Jade spread her arms. "What I've got on. He's picking me up here after work."

"Still, you can't go, you know, looking any old way. I'll watch the store. You go home and at least put on fresh makeup."

"Terri—"

"Besides, you can't leave Mocha here all night. You *have* to take him home and feed him." Her friend had a point there.

"Okay. I'll leave at about three."

Terri looked smug, but Jade didn't have time to comment on it because Greta walked in.

"Hidey-ho, darlins. I'm here to knit." She looked from one of them to the other. "What have I missed? What's going on?"

"Jade has herself a date with the handsome pet shop guy this evening," said Terri.

Jade glared at Terri, but the look was wasted. Terri wasn't even paying attention.

"Well, yee-haw!" Greta exclaimed. "Good on ya. Where are you going?"

"I have no idea," said Jade. "It's not that big a deal."

"It'd be a big deal to me. I'd make sure I was wearing my best underclothes just in case," said Greta, with a wink.

"In case you got lucky?" Terri asked.

"Or died from the excitement of being on a date with Hottie McHot-hot."

Jade ran a hand over her flushed face. "Terri tells me you guys are making great strides on the party planning front."

"Oh, yes, we are. And, Terri, I spoke with Sandra earlier, and she's just as pleased as punch with the way things are lining up. She's agreed to give us two cash prizes for the bingo game—a one-hundred-fifty-dollar prize and then, the last prize of the night, a five-hundred-dollar prize."

"That's fantastic!" Terri gave Greta a hug. "Are either of us eligible to play for prizes?"

"By crackies, we'd better be. I intend to play. Don't you?"

"I sure do," said Terri.

"Another thing—that sexy reporter Mitch Reedy from the news will be here to talk to us on Friday," said Greta. "And if we do a good enough job of talking it up, he might come back and cover the actual event on Saturday. I'm already working on what I'm going to say."

Caleb arrived at Nothin' But Knit just before five-thirty that afternoon. When Jade looked up and saw him, her mouth got dry and her legs turned to lead. He really was gorgeous. And he was taking her out on a date. But *why* was he taking her out on a date? Men like him didn't date women like her. Jittery Jade got dates with guys who were awkward and nervous, just like she was.

He was dressed casually—still wearing the jeans and shirt he wore earlier—but he was every bit as impressive as if he wore a perfectly tailored suit. The white polo he wore really showed off his muscular arms. Dark blue jeans looked lived in but accentuated his strong thighs. She could only imagine what they did for his butt. Jade was glad she hadn't changed her clothes—her jeans and pale blue sleeveless embroidered shirt was fine for this date—but she was relieved that she'd taken the time to reapply her makeup.

Caleb held up the picnic basket he carried in his right hand. "Millie let me borrow this. And I filled it at the café. Are you up for a picnic?"

"Sure."

Terri came up and clapped Jade on the back. "You two have fun. I'll lock up."

Jade turned to look at Terri, who waited until Caleb was looking in the other direction to fan her face with her hand.

"Ready?" Caleb asked.

No. "Uh, yeah," she said.

He led her out to a red Jeep in the parking lot. He unlocked the doors and put the picnic basket on the back seat.

"You know, I could drive myself." It occurred that she didn't know this man at all. Should she really be getting into a vehicle with him?

"Um…you don't have to, unless you think I'm a bad driver or something." Caleb gave her a hard look. "Do I need references?"

"No. I'm sorry." She climbed into the passenger side of the Jeep.

As they drove, Jade kept her eyes glued on the scenery outside her window. She didn't want to look at Caleb's sexy profile, to notice the tiny bit of hair beneath his right cheek that he'd missed when he was shaving this morning, to think about how long and dark his eyelashes were, to wonder how that hand on the steering wheel would feel cupping her face.

"Do you like the lake?" he asked.

"I do," she said, still refusing to look at him. "Is that where we're going?"

"Yep. I have a boat I keep stored out there. I thought that's where we'd have our picnic."

"That sounds nice."

He blew out a breath. "Look, if you've changed your mind, I'll turn around, and we'll go back to the Community Center."

"No." She finally looked at him. "I'm just a little tired, that's all."

"Rough day?"

"A little. After lunch, it was a madhouse. Who knew we would be so busy on a Monday? But, that's a good thing, right?"

"Always, in my opinion," said Caleb.

Jade was able to settle her nerves and engage in small talk like a regular human being until they arrived at the lake. Caleb parked at the marina, got the picnic basket out of the backseat, and then came around and opened her door.

"I might need your help with the boat." He placed the picnic basket at her feet. "Be right back."

She watched as he went over to a storage unit, unlocked it, and raised the door. He dragged a five-person pedal boat out of the unit and closed the door. Then he bent down and hoisted the boat onto his back.

"Can you carry the picnic basket?" he asked.

"Yes." She laughed as she carried the basket over to him. "This is your boat?"

"Yeah. Don't you like it? I never said it was a yacht."

"You never said it was a pedal boat either."

"I don't recall your asking." He went to the edge of the water and put down the boat. "But I did say I might need your help with it." He put the basket into the boat, turned, and held out his hand.

Jade placed her hand in his. It felt as warm and as strong as she knew it would. She gingerly stepped into the boat and sat down. A giggle bubbled up inside her. "I haven't been on a pedal boat since I was in middle school."

"Then you're in for a treat." Caleb climbed in beside her, turned the boat out toward the lake, and began to pedal.

Jade pedaled too—she was glad she'd worn sneakers today—and soon they were in the middle of the lake. "Where are we going to eat?"

"There's a cove—" He pointed. "Just over there."

She saw the shady cove, surrounded by laurels. Caleb steered them in that direction.

"It's beautiful out here," she said.

"It is. It's one of my favorite places to come and just...be." He chuckled. "Doesn't that sound all existential?"

"Maybe. But I know what you mean."

They stopped the boat in the cove, and Caleb reached around Jade for the picnic basket. He'd brought an assortment of sandwiches—chicken salad, ham, turkey, and roast beef—chips, cookies, chocolate-dipped strawberries, and a thermos of iced tea.

"This is way too much food," Jade said.

"I know. But I didn't know what you'd like. I figure this way, there's bound to be something here you'll like."

"Actually, I like it all."

"What a coincidence! Me too." He peered into the basket. "I do see one thing I forgot. An extra cup. We'll have to share the one that came with the thermos." He looked up, his dark eyes meeting hers. "Is that all right?"

She nodded, feeling breathless and tongue-tied at his nearness again.

"So, tell me five things about Jade Burt that I'd be surprised to know," said Caleb.

"Um, that's kind of a toughie." She grinned. "It might require food for thought." She dug into the picnic basket and brought out a chicken salad sandwich.

"I've got all night and plenty of food."

She unwrapped the sandwich and took a self-conscious bite. He got himself a turkey sandwich.

Jade realized Caleb was looking at her expectantly. "This is delicious."

"This one is too. Have you thought of your first little-known Jade fact yet?"

"I won the sixth-grade spelling bee."

"What was the winning word?" he asked.

"*Mischievous.* Does that count as my second fact?"

"Nope."

"Tell you what—I'll trade you fact for fact. Give me a little-known Caleb fact."

"All right." He took a bite of his sandwich and opened a mini bag of chips. "You already know I'm the captain of a boat." He offered her the chips, and she took one. "And that I pack a mean picnic."

"True. So, tell me what draws you to my grandmother."

"Ah. You're worried about the other woman in my life. Is that it?" He took the cap off the thermos and poured the cup full of tea. He offered her the first drink, but she declined. "She reminds me of my own grandmother—kind, thoughtful, classy…a little out there."

"Sounds like you're close."

"We were. She passed last April."

"I'm sorry," Jade said.

"Me too. I miss her every day." He took a drink of the tea. "Next Jade fact please."

"I can play harmonica."

"No way!"

She laughed. "I can. My grandpa taught me when I was a little girl, and I just kept it up."

"Millie's husband?"

"No, my grandpa on my dad's side."

He nodded.

"What?" she asked. "You can't see my grandma with a blues-playing harmonica man?"

"No. I imagine if Millie's husband played an instrument, it would be piano or maybe saxophone."

"You've really got her up on a pedestal, haven't you?"

"Why not? After all, she led me to you."

"Okay, that was super cheesy." Jade laughed.

"I know. But I thought it was a good try."

She inclined her head. "It was."

"Stuff like that goes over really well with the golden oldies."

"Ah-ha. Is that your target demographic?" she asked.

"Only when they come in to buy pet supplies." Caleb leaned back and studied her. "Is that why you think I'm nice to your grandma? Do you think I'm just a flirt or something?"

"You *are* a flirt. You can't help yourself."

He turned down the corners of his mouth in silent agreement. "But there's a difference in flirting and having serious intentions."

Jade wondered what his intentions were about her—if there were any—but she was afraid to ask.

After eating their fill, they pedaled around the lake some more. Jade learned three of the five little-known facts about Caleb: he was a wiz at solving cryptograms, he received academic and baseball partial scholarships to attend college, and he played Freddy in a high-school theater production of *Pygmalion*. In addition to his discovering that she'd won a spelling bee and that she played harmonica, Caleb had cajoled Jade into confessing that she'd once made herself a teddy bear out of her mother's bath rug.

"Two more facts to go," Caleb reminded her, as she watched a bass swim past.

"Okay. After the infamous teddy bear incident, I learned to knit so I wouldn't be tempted to channel my crafty desires into destroying the household linens."

"Crafty desires. I like the sound of that." He smirked.

Jade could feel the heat rise in her cheeks and turned her face away. "I still have my bath rug bear, by the way. He's packed away at my mom's house."

"Has he held up well?"

"Not terribly. But, in my defense, he was never put together very well in the first place. Bath mat material is hard to sew, especially for a seven-year-old."

"So you've been knitting since you were seven?"

She nodded. "That's why it seemed only natural to open a knitting shop. I wanted to do something I truly had a passion for. Unfortunately, my mother believes I'll wind up falling on my face."

"Nah. Nothin' But Knit gets a ton of traffic, and it'll pick up even more after the grand opening celebration this weekend."

"I hope so. But enough about that. It's your turn. Why did you choose to go into urban and regional planning?"

"I never could understand why so many resources are wasted. Why abandon a deserted shopping mall just to build a new one five miles away? I decided to try to do something about it—to make a difference somehow." He shrugged. "I'd like to think I'm part visionary, part preservationist, and part resource manager."

"That's...noble. I imagine then that, when you've earned your graduate degree, you'll be heading off to somewhere far more exciting than Kinsey Falls."

"Not necessarily. Look at the Community Center. That building was a brilliant use of resources."

"True." Still, there'd been only one dying mall in Kinsey Falls. What was left—or would be left—to lend itself to regional planning by the time Caleb finished school? Jade felt sure Caleb would leave once he realized the area's career limitations.

She hadn't realized she'd stopped pedaling until Caleb asked if she was getting tired.

"What? No. I'm fine," she said.

"Still, we should probably bring this vessel in to shore." He steered the boat toward the marina. "Thank you for coming. I've enjoyed this."

"So have I."

"Since you owe me one last fact, what's your favorite flavor of ice cream?" Caleb asked.

"Chocolate—the chocolatier the better. Yours?"

"Mint chocolate chip." He pointed toward a small, gabled building painted in bright pink and yellow, with pastel blue trim. "Let's go treat ourselves to our favorites to top off the evening."

After putting the boat back in the storage unit, Caleb slipped his hand into hers and escorted her to the ice cream parlor. Jade enjoyed holding Caleb's hand. He'd clasped hers casually, but the touch had made her feel warm, thrilled, and protected all at once.

When they had their ice cream cones, they walked back outside to a picnic table on a knob overlooking the lake. There they ate their ice cream while the sky turned shades of orange and yellow and the sun dipped into the water.

Chapter Eight

ON TUESDAY MORNING, MILLIE didn't know who she wanted to talk with first—Jade or Caleb. She was terrified she might learn that Jade had the time of her life while Caleb felt the date hadn't gone well. If she talked with Caleb first and he seemed disappointed with the date, how could Millie feign ignorance of that if Jade was now head over heels for the guy? After all, Jade wasn't known to date much, period. And, to Millie's knowledge, she'd never dated a man like Caleb Young.

Millie herself had only ever dated one man like Caleb, and she'd married him. Jade's mother, on the other hand, had dated quite a few men like Caleb but had ultimately thrown them over to marry the toad—Jade's father—and later the snake. Fiona was again divorced and was dating what could only be described in Millie's mind as the lizard. She said a silent prayer asking God's forgiveness for her malignment of reptiles and poured herself a second cup of coffee. Her ringing phone wound up making her decision of who to talk with first. A short time later, Millie was in such a hurry to get to the pet shop that she took the elevator. As soon as the doors opened, she barreled down the hall to Hightail It! Caleb was standing at the register, and thankfully, there were no customers in the store at the moment.

"Good morning, Millie. You look beautiful as always." He drew his brows together. "Although you're a little flushed. Are you feeling okay?"

"I'm fine," she said, dispensing with small talk. "Geri called."

"Is everything all right?" Caleb came out from behind the counter and placed a hand on her shoulder. "Do you need to sit down?"

She waved away his concerns. "Perry is fine. In fact, another baby possum around the same age—Geri says he's ten to eleven weeks—was brought in last night."

"Is that a good thing or a bad thing?"

"It's good. They'll have each other. Geri told me they'd be released back into the wild together."

"That's great news then. Perry won't have to wander alone. What's the newbie's name?"

"I asked, but Geri said they don't name animals—or in any other way treat them as pets—when they're releasing them back into the wild. I don't even think she calls Perry by name."

Caleb arched a dark brow. "What's the other possum's name, Millie? I know you've given it one."

"Parker."

He gave her a one-armed hug. "Did Geri say when Perry and Parker will move on to the next leg of their adventure?"

"The end of September is when they're scheduled to be released." She smiled. "And she said if we want to come, we can watch the release from a short distance away."

"Want to come? We wouldn't miss it!" He grinned. "Maybe we can pack up that picnic basket and take it with us. Thanks again for letting me borrow it. I'll get it back to you right after work today."

"No rush. But, um, speaking of the picnic basket, how did the date go?"

"Great." He smiled over top of Millie's head at the couple walking into the shop. "Hi and welcome to Hightail It! Is there anything I can help you find?"

He might've been saved by his customers this time, but she'd get some answers when he returned her picnic basket.

* * *

The more nonchalant her grandmother tried to appear, the more transparent she was to Jade. The woman was dying to get details about the date with Caleb. And of course, Terri was right there with her. But Jade had resisted dishing to her best friend, and she wasn't planning on telling Millie anything either.

Then Millie said this: "I was just over at Hightail It! telling Caleb about my conversation with Geri."

Jade's spine stiffened. Millie had been to the pet shop. Talking with Caleb. Had Caleb mentioned their date?

"Isn't that wonderful?" Millie was saying.

Blinking, Jade focused her eyes back on her grandmother. *What's supposed to be wonderful?* She'd completely zoned out. But it apparently had something to do with the baby possum, and Grandma thought it was wonderful. So Jade pasted on a smile and said, "Yes! Yes, it *is* wonderful!"

Millie crossed her arms. "What's wonderful?"

"That Perry is doing so well," Jade guessed. She glanced at Terri for confirmation.

Terri gave Jade a brief nod, but Millie still wasn't buying it.

"I know you weren't listening, Jade. Once I said *Caleb*, your eyes glazed over."

Terri grinned and leaned in closer. It was obvious she thought Millie had Jade's back to the wall and that Jade was finally going to have to tell them about her date. But Jade was determined not to give anything away.

The date had been fun and romantic and, other than the hand-holding, completely platonic. When they'd gotten back to the Community Center, Caleb had walked her to her car but hadn't made any move to kiss her goodnight.

What did it mean? That he didn't enjoy himself? That he hadn't found her attractive? That he wasn't planning on asking her out again? That he didn't get the impression she liked him? That he'd only taken her out to prove to her that he was a good guy? Just what was it?

Of course, Jade had told herself from the very start that guys like Caleb didn't date girls like her. But, deep down, she'd hoped she'd been wrong about that.

She realized Millie and Terri were staring at her. "Um, what? I'm sorry. I got distracted. We're going to need to replenish our supply of yarn soon. I'd better get on that."

"Humph. I was going to ask how your date with Caleb went," said Millie. "Since you're incapable of coherent thought this morning, it must've gone incredibly well." She turned to Terri. "Please don't let her embarrass herself in front of the customers today."

"I'll do my best."

Jade ignored their banter and took a barcode scanner over to the shelves of yarn. A sudden thought stopped her in her tracks. "Grandma!"

Millie looked back over her shoulder.

"Don't discuss me or my date...with *anyone*. I'm begging you."

Millie gave her a solemn nod before going out the door.

"She's right," Terri said. "That must've been some date."

* * *

No longer in a rush, Millie took the stairs and went to see Greta. She knocked on the door and was glad when Greta answered right away.

"Honey, are you all right?" Greta asked, ushering Millie into the living room. "Your little possum didn't die, did it?"

"No, I got a call this morning, and Perry is doing well. It's Jade I'm concerned about."

"Why? Didn't she go out with that gorgeous pet shop clerk yesterday evening?"

Millie nodded. "And I can't get anything about it out of either of them. But Jade is as spaced-out as she can be today." She sighed. "What if she fell head over heels for Caleb, and he didn't like her?"

Greta sank onto the sofa. "It could be the other way around," she said, as Millie sat beside her. "Maybe he liked her, and she didn't like him. He could be a sloppy kisser or something." She scrunched up her nose. "No, I take that back. I imagine he's a terrific kisser. He'd wrap those big, strong arms around a woman, brush her hair back off her cheek, and then—"

"Greta!"

"What?"

"I shouldn't have gotten involved. I've never tried to fix my granddaughter up in her life—until now—and I'd bet you dollars to doughnuts that beautiful, charming Caleb has swept Jade right off her feet."

"Possibly. I'd go so far as to say probably. But, Millie, even if he has swept her off her feet, how do you know he hasn't fallen for her too?"

"I don't."

"Then chill. Make sure you have all the facts before you spazz." Greta got up and strode over to the kitchen. "I *know* I have problems...and I have to get them fixed before Friday. Want some hibiscus tea?"

"Sure, I'll try it. What problems are you having?"

"Well, back when Sandra tapped Terri and me to help with planning this grand opening shindig, Terri and I thought we could draw a bigger crowd by renting tables to local vendors." She filled her bright red tea kettle with water, placed it on the stove, and turned on the burner. "Also, renting out those spaces would give us more money to work with."

"How did Sandra feel about that?"

"She thought it was a swell idea until some of the retailers got wind of it and said they were afraid some of the vendors would take business away from them. Now Terri and I—or rather, I, since Terri is working—get the glorious job of having the retailers okay the vendors...or not."

"What sort of vendors are we talking about?" Millie asked.

The tea kettle whistled, and Greta prepared their tea. She brought the pot and two cups over on a tray. "I don't usually put sweetener in mine. If you need some, let me know."

"All right. You were telling me about the vendors?"

"Oh, yeah. Well, we didn't sign anybody up that we thought would be in direct competition with the storeowners. There are two or three authors, someone selling essential oils, a jewelry maker, and a woodcarver."

"If you need any help, I'll be happy to pitch in." Millie tasted the tea. "Oh, gee. This is a lot better than I thought it would be."

"You'll really help me?" Greta asked.

"Of course. I'll be happy to do it."

Millie volunteered to talk with the vendors on the right side of the hallway. It would give her a chance to see Caleb again—with a legitimate reason for being there—and this time, she would come right out and ask him about the date.

She started at the back of the mall and worked her way toward Hightail It! After getting someone at the pet supply store to sign off on the vendor roster, she could pop in and see Jade, provided she got a favorable date report from Caleb.

The person manning the register was not Caleb.

"Hello! Welcome to Hightail It!" said the bespectacled young man. "I'm Aidan. Is there anything I can help you find?"

"Are you the manager?"

"No, ma'am. That'd be Caleb. He's around here somewhere with Adalyn. I'll call him up here for you."

"That's all right. I don't want to bother him while he's with a customer," Millie said. "I'll look around until he's finished with her."

The color rose in Aidan's cheeks. "Adalyn's not a customer and… Well, they could be a while."

"I've got a few minutes." Millie walked over to the pet collars and fingered them as if she actually had a pet and was considering buying a collar. *Who was this Adalyn, and what did she mean to Caleb? Whatever the nature of their relationship, it was enough to make Aidan blush.*

Hearing muted voices—one of which definitely belonged to Caleb—in the storeroom, Millie hazarded a peek at Aidan. He was staring down at his phone, so she eased into the storeroom.

Caleb was standing with his back to Millie. All she could see of the girl presumed to be Adalyn were the pretty, manicured hands currently splayed across Caleb's broad shoulders. The couple wasn't kissing, but that was no sign they hadn't been.

Judging by Adalyn's bubblegum pink nails, it was a safe bet she was wearing lipstick. Millie had an urgent need to know if any of it had been transferred to Caleb.

She cleared her throat.

Caleb turned, and his eyes widened when he saw her. He also quickly dropped his arms from around Adalyn's waist. "Millie! Hi!"

Millie looked from Caleb to Adalyn and back. She wore pale pink lip gloss. He did not. So, at least, he had *that* going for him at the moment.

"I'm sorry to interrupt," Millie said.

"You're not." He looked down at the adorable blonde beside him. "This is Adalyn. Adalyn, Millie."

"Hello." Adalyn gave Millie the briefest of smiles and then turned back to Caleb.

"I'll talk to you later, Caleb, when you're not in the middle of something." Millie turned and hurried out of the store and upstairs to her apartment.

Chapter Nine

CALEB WAS SLIGHTLY WINDED when he rushed into Nothin' But Knit. Jade was finishing up with a customer, and she held up one finger to let him know she'd be with him in a second. He paced back and forth in front of the pegboard displaying various sizes of knitting needles.

Jade was glad he'd stopped by to see her, but seeing his agitated state concerned her. She went over to him as soon as her customer left. "What's wrong?"

"It's Millie. Have you spoken with her within the past half hour or so?"

"No. Why?"

"Does she have a habit of not answering her phone?"

"No." Jade's heart rate was ramping up. "I've got to get to her apartment."

"That might not be necessary." Caleb looked down at the floor. "I believe she's upset with me, and that's why she's not answering my calls. So, call first, and if she answers, we'll know she's okay."

"Why would she be upset with you?"

"We'll talk about it after we're sure she's all right. Please."

Jade took out her phone and called Millie. Her grandmother answered on the first ring. "Grandma, is anything wrong?"

"No," said Millie. "Why would you think that?"

"Caleb said he's been trying to call you but that you haven't picked up."

"I'm fine, just busy. I'll talk with Caleb—and you—later. Both of you need to get back to work."

Jade ended the call and turned to see that Caleb had discovered Mocha and was sitting on the bench by the window cradling the cat.

She sat with them. "That's weird. Mocha typically doesn't warm up to strangers so quickly."

"Mocha is an excellent judge of character." Caleb smiled at Jade.

"What did you do to upset Grandma?"

He looked around the shop.

"Don't worry," Jade said. "Terri is in the knitting room with a couple of our regulars. Now, what did you do to Grandma?"

"She came into Hightail It! and saw me hugging my ex-girlfriend."

"Oh." Jade lifted Mocha off Caleb's lap and placed him on her own.

"No, not 'oh.' It's nothing like that. Adalyn's family lives in Greenville, South Carolina, and she found out this morning that her uncle died. She needed a shoulder to cry on—that's it."

"I'm sorry about her uncle. Will you be driving her to South Carolina then?"

"Of course not. I agree she shouldn't be driving as upset as she is, but her dad is on his way to get her." He stood. "I need to get back. I just wanted to make sure Millie was all right."

"Thanks."

He left, but Jade remained on the bench holding Mocha. As she stroked the cat's soft fur, she examined everything Caleb had said. He was hugging his ex because she was distraught over the death of a family member. That was reasonable. It certainly didn't mean either of them wanted to get back together.

On the other hand, Caleb hadn't taken the opportunity to mention that he'd enjoyed their date. Nor had he asked her out again. Was he waiting on some cue from her? After all, she'd acted as if she hadn't been interested in him at all prior to their date. Or was he simply not interested?

* * *

After he got off work, Caleb returned the picnic basket. Millie opened the door, took the basket, and said, "Come on in. Did you go see Jade to do damage control?"

"Not at all. When you didn't answer my call, I was concerned about you." He nodded toward the basket. "Thanks again for letting me borrow that. I think the picnic was a success."

"Do you?"

"Yes. At least, that's the impression I got."

They were standing in the living room, and Millie invited Caleb to sit down. He took a seat on the armchair, and after placing the picnic basket on the kitchen table, she sank onto the sofa.

"It's apparent you're upset with me," Caleb said.

"I'm not upset with you. I think you're a wonderful young man. But I don't want my granddaughter getting hurt."

"I don't want that either."

Their eyes locked as if they were trying to read each other's minds.

Caleb broke their gaze. "What did you need to see me about earlier?"

Millie explained that she was helping Greta by taking a list of proposed vendors around to Community Center retailers for their approval or disapproval. She got the list and handed it to Caleb.

He read over it and then initialed the form. "I think having these other vendors come in will only enhance the celebration and bring more attention to all of us. Don't you?"

"I do. I believe the celebration will be a lot of fun and that we should go all out so that the Community Center can benefit from some great publicity."

"Me too." He grinned. "Will you quit being mad at me?"

"I was never mad at you." She leaned forward with her elbows on her knees. "I'd never been so impressed with a young man that I'd tried to fix him up with Jade. Until I met you."

"You didn't fix us up though. We met because of you...and Perry, but you didn't arrange a blind date or anything. I asked Jade out, and she accepted."

"Are you glad about that?"

"I am."

Millie sat back in her chair. "What about the girl in the storeroom who was holding on to you for dear life?"

"Adalyn had a death in the family. She came to me because she needed someone to lean on."

She smiled. "You're smart enough to realize that some women will use any excuse they can find to get into a man's arms."

"She might want that, but I don't. Whether things work out with Jade or not, Adalyn is out of my life."

* * *

Before going home for the day, Jade went up to check on Millie. True, she'd spoken with her grandma earlier, but angry or not, it wasn't like Millie to ignore a phone call. Even though she had a key to Millie's apartment, she'd only use it in an emergency. She knocked and was relieved when Millie promptly answered the door.

"Grandma, hi. Are you sure you're feeling okay?"

"I'm fine." Millie moved back, allowing Jade to come inside and put Mocha and his cat carrier on the floor. "I'm sorry if I worried you."

"It's just that, even if you were ticked at Caleb, I can't imagine you not answering his calls."

"I must've dozed off. I didn't even realize he'd been trying to reach me until you called." Millie walked over to the kitchen, and Jade followed her. "You're probably hungry. Would you like me to make us something?"

"No. I appreciate the offer, but I need to get Mocha home and get him fed."

Upon hearing his name, Mocha let out a plaintive meow.

"I might have some tuna," Millie said.

"We're fine, Grandma, really. I only came to make sure you're feeling all right."

"I'm fit as a fiddle." She nodded at the picnic basket sitting on the table. "Caleb brought that back. In fact, he hadn't been gone ten minutes when you got here."

"Did he say anything about...you know...about the picnic?"

"He seemed to feel that it went well. What do you think?"

"I believe it did." And Jade *did* believe that. Up until the part where he hadn't kissed her. "He explained what you saw in the storeroom, by the way. That girl—Adalyn—had learned about the death of her uncle and needed a shoulder to cry on."

Millie opened the refrigerator and took out a pitcher of tea. "Yeah, he told me. And I told *him* that some women will use any excuse to get close to a man." She got a tumbler from the cabinet. "Want some tea?"

"No. I really do need to be getting home, Grandma." She kissed Millie's cheek. "Get some rest this evening."

"Okay, sweetie, I will. And, Jade?"

Jade stopped halfway to the door and looked back at her grandmother. "Yeah?"

"If you want that man, you'd better let him know it. Because if you don't want him, someone else does."

* * *

78

By the time Greta came over to get Millie's half of the retail shop approvals, Millie had already taken her bath and slipped into her favorite pajamas. They were mint green with tiny white polka dots.

"Mercy sakes, Millie, are you sick?"

"No, I'm not sick. Unless you count my being sick of everybody asking me if I'm all right today. I wanted to get comfy, that's all."

"Who else is asking after your health?" Greta asked.

"Caleb and Jade. He's the one who started it. He apparently called, and I'd dozed off or something and missed it. So, he went and told Jade and got her all worried."

"Well, it's not like you to take naps." Greta slipped her shoes off and put her feet up on the ottoman in front of the armchair. "How'd their date go?"

"Neither one of them was eager to discuss it with me, but I think it must've gone fairly well," Millie said. "Do you happen to know a YP named Adalyn?"

Greta shook her head. "Name doesn't ring a bell. Why?"

"I believe she's the girl Caleb used to date. Today she found out that a relative died and needed to find comfort in Caleb's arms in the Hightail It! storeroom." Millie pressed her lips together and raised her eyebrows.

"No easier way into a man's arms than to shed a few tears."

"That's what I said."

"I'll nose around and see what I can find out about this girl," Greta said. "You say her name is Adalyn?"

"That's her—pretty little blonde."

"I'd bet Kelsey knows her. Kelsey makes it her business to know everything, everybody, and everything *about* everybody."

* * *

Driving home, Jade's conversation with Millie kept going through her head. Maybe her grandma was right about Adalyn using her grief as a way to get back into Caleb's life. Jade had never been one to employ any sort of calculated tactics to get a man. But one thing Millie had said resonated with Jade more than anything else.

If you want that man, you'd better let him know it.

Jade's phone was connected to the Bluetooth in her car, and she and Caleb had exchanged numbers last night. Before she could chicken out, she called him.

"Hello."

At the sound of his deep, sexy voice, she nearly ended the call. But she didn't. For one thing, he'd know it was her and that she was a pitiful coward. Besides, one way or the other, she needed to know if Caleb was interested in her.

"Would you let me make you dinner tomorrow night?" she asked.

"Yeah," he said. "I'd love that."

"Good. You can, um…follow me home from the Community Center. If that's all right."

"If I follow you home, will you keep me?"

She knew he was making a joke, but his words conjured up all sorts of images and feelings.

"Jade?"

"Yes. I mean…I might."

He chuckled. "I'll look forward to it."

Chapter Ten

JADE SCROLLED THROUGH RECIPE after recipe. She didn't cook very often and wasn't terribly confident in her culinary abilities. She needed to find something delicious but easy to make. Nothing she'd come across so far fit the bill. She closed her laptop and called Terri.

"I did the stupidest thing," Jade said when her friend answered.

"What did you do?"

"I called and invited Caleb here for dinner tomorrow night. And he accepted."

"Jade, that's awesome! It's definitely not stupid. I'm proud of you."

"Thanks, but I have to come up with something I can actually cook. You know I'm not the world's best chef."

"No one ever said you had to be. How about spaghetti and meatballs?" Terri suggested. "You could get frozen meatballs and store-bought sauce and put them in a slow cooker, put the spaghetti on to boil when you got home, and *voila*!"

"But what if he doesn't like spaghetti?"

"Who doesn't like spaghetti? But if you're worried about it, call him and ask."

"No," Jade said. "I can't do that—it'd be embarrassing."

"I disagree, but if you don't want to call him, tell me what he brought on your picnic."

Jade told her.

"Okay, so you know he likes turkey. Make turkey."

"I don't have time to roast a turkey!"

"You aren't going to *roast* a turkey. You're going to put a turkey breast in the slow cooker and let it cook all day," Terri told her. "You're going to pick up rolls and sides from the grocery store where you buy the turkey breast, and you're going to stop stressing."

"That sounds great, but even though Grandma did leave me a lot of her cooking stuff when she moved to the Community Center, including her slow cooker, I don't know the first thing about cooking a turkey breast in one."

"I'll email you a recipe."

"But—"

"Stop. It."

Jade expelled a breath. "I'm nervous."

"I know, but you'll be all right. You took care of the main thing—you invited the man over."

"Right. You're right. Now, if I can just keep from giving him food poisoning."

"Enough with the negative thinking," Terri said. "Go to the grocery store first thing tomorrow morning and get what you need. I'll take care of everything here."

"Okay. But I'll be in as soon as I can."

"Take your time. I'm perfectly capable of managing Nothin' But Knit on my own for a little while."

"I know you are. I just don't want to take advantage of your generosity."

"You're not taking advantage. Hopefully, you'll have to run the store on your own sometime while I prepare for an amazing date with some gorgeous guy."

Jade laughed. "I hope so too."

After ending the call, she opened her email and read the recipe Terri had sent. It didn't seem terribly difficult. Jade felt confident she could at least get the turkey breast prepped and in the slow cooker properly. And she could pick up rolls and sides at the deli counter like Terri had suggested…and she could get the ingredients for a peanut butter chocolate poke cake for dessert. Grandma always took it to church functions, and it was a huge hit. It was called a poke cake because the baker poked holes into it and poured the icing over the top.

On to problem number two: what was she going to wear?

The next morning, Jade slept through her six-a.m. alarm. In fact, she didn't wake up until seven, when Mocha hopped onto the bed to meow directly into her face. Upon looking at the clock, Jade immediately leapt from the bed and threw herself into a frenzy of activity. She fed the cat, readied the coffee pot, took a shower, got dressed, poured herself a cup of coffee, and answered her ringing phone.

"Calm down," Terri's firm voice instructed.

"I am calm."

"You're anything but."

"Okay, fine. I'm freaking out. But how do you know that?" Jade asked.

"Because we've been friends over half our lives. Take a deep breath and hold it to the count of four." Terri waited. "Now let that breath out slowly. And do it again."

Jade did as she was told, willing her heart to stop racing. "Terri, what if—"

"Nope," Terri interrupted. "We're not *what iffing* today. We have a plan—one that doesn't include second-guessing everything we do—and we're sticking to that plan."

"I know but—"

"Are you dressed and ready to go?"

Jade looked down at her t-shirt and jeans. "Kinda."

"Are you on your way to the store?"

"Not yet, b—"

"Then get your butt in the car, woman."

"Thanks," she said, with a laugh. "I'll be there as soon as I can."

"Take your time. This is going to be a good night. I know it."

Jade wished she could feel as sure as Terri seemed to.

* * *

Greta came to see Millie as soon as she'd finished her walk. Millie, still a little groggy even after her second cup of coffee, was watching the morning news. She turned off the television when Greta came to sit with her in the living room.

"You're still looking a smidge peaked," Greta said, sitting on the sofa and peering at Millie. "Are you certain you're not coming down with some kind of bug?"

"I'm fine, Greta. Have you found something out about Adalyn already?"

"Of course, I have. I walked with Kelsey this morning. And like I've already told you, Kelsey knows stuff on everybody."

"What stuff does she know on Adalyn?"

"Adalyn and Caleb got together right after they both moved here," Greta said. "Apparently, they were seeing each other about every day. Kelsey said Caleb put the brakes on because Adalyn got too clingy."

"Well, by the looks of her in the Hightail It! storeroom yesterday, she's still clingy."

Greta nodded. "Kelsey said Adalyn fought the break up and keeps trying to win Caleb back. She told me she never got the impression Caleb was as head over heels for Adalyn as she was for him." She tilted her head. "I got the feeling that if Kelsey didn't have her cap set for Justin, she'd be after Caleb."

"Well, don't tell Kelsey I said so, but she and Adalyn can both hit the road and go to bouncing. Caleb is Jade's. I hope."

84

* * *

When Jade got home from the grocery store, she made the rub for the turkey breast using olive oil, garlic powder, salt, pepper, and paprika. She rubbed the mixture onto both sides of the turkey and then washed her hands. Following the recipe's instructions, she cut an onion and a garlic clove in half and placed them on the bottom of the slow cooker to flavor the meat and to keep the turkey breast from poaching in its own liquid.

After putting the turkey into the slow cooker, Jade washed her hands yet again and made the chocolate cake. While the cake was baking, she placed two white taper candles in the crystal candle holders she'd found in Millie's china cabinet the night before. She put the candles in the center of the dining room table and placed a box of matches nearby so she wouldn't be scrambling to find something to light the candles with when the time came.

She then stepped over Mocha for the umpteenth time and went into the bedroom to second-guess her outfit again. She finally settled on an outfit she felt was sexy but that she could comfortably work in for the rest of the day—a wispy white eyelet lace dress and nude wedge sandals.

The oven timer dinged, and Jade hurried to the kitchen to take out the cake. She put the pan on a wire rack to cool and then made the peanut butter mixture to go on top. As soon as the cake was adequately cooled, she used the handle of a wooden spoon to poke holes in the sheet cake and then spread the peanut butter icing across the top. She'd finish up with the chocolate syrup and peanut butter cup candies before serving.

Jade felt so very accomplished and proud of herself. She was doing this. She was actually doing it! And she was calm!

Her calmness was actually denial. She made it almost all the way to Nothin' But Knit before she had to pull over to the side of the road and throw up in a ditch. Fortunately, she didn't soil her dress or her shoes. Unfortunately, she didn't know how she was going to make it through the rest of her work day, much less her dinner date.

Mocha went straight to his bed beneath the counter when Jade opened the door to the pet carrier. Always sensitive to her moods, he knew something was off about her today.

"Excuse me, Terri." Jade's voice came out raspy, and she cleared her throat. "Do you have any mints?"

Terri hurried over from the yarn bins with an armload of yellow angora. She looked around to make sure there were no customers in the shop before saying, "You threw up, didn't you?"

Jade nodded.

Terri put the yarn on the counter, grabbed her purse, and rifled around until she retrieved half a pack of breath mints. "Here. They're peppermint, so they'll help calm your stomach."

"Thanks."

"You look beautiful. This evening is going to be great."

"Sure…yeah." She pointed toward the yarn. "What's that for?"

"Some woman called a few minutes ago and said she needed ten skeins of yellow angora. I hope this is the shade she wants."

"Me too. That's an excellent sale."

"I know." Terri gently took Jade by the shoulders and pushed her away from the counter. "Don't puke on it."

Jade huffed. "I won't."

Terri arched a brow.

"Fine." Jade wandered into the knitting room to see if there was anything she needed to do in there. No. It was spotless. She decided to clean the table anyway. It couldn't hurt, and she was desperate for a distraction.

"Hidey-ho!"

Jade smiled. *Ah, the call of the purple-plumed golden oldie—the perfect distraction.*

"Hey, Greta," she said, strolling back into the main part of the store.

"Hey, yourself, darlin'. Don't you look pretty as a picture?"

"Thank you. You look awfully nice yourself." Greta wore navy capris, a red-and-white striped shirt, and white canvas sneakers with red laces. "What's going on?"

"I'm here to run an idea by you gals. It's for the celebration on Saturday."

"Greta, it's too late for us to add anything else," Terri said. "The celebration is in two days."

"Technically three. But that's beside the point. When the flyers were posted about this bash, we never said exactly what—" Greta made air quotes. "—*fun and games for the whole family* we were doing. So, check out my idea." She raised her palms. "Dance contest."

"Dance contest?" Jade echoed.

Greta grinned. "Dance contest. Think about it, Terri. You've been wanting to pit the golden oldies against the VPs. What better way to do it?"

"I never said I was trying to *pit* anyone against anyone. You make me sound like I'm running a gladiator match." Terri looked from Greta to Jade. "What I said was that we need to be sure to *include* both groups."

"And this will do that exceptionally well," Greta said. "We'll play music from several decades, and the couples have to be able to dance to all of it."

Terri opened her mouth to speak, but an elegant woman with dark brown hair shot through with flecks of silver strode through the door and up to the counter.

"Pardon me, ladies, but I called earlier about ten skeins of yellow angora?"

"Yes." Terri picked up a skein of the yarn. "Is this the color you had in mind?"

As the woman told Terri the shade was perfect, Jade led Greta over to the bench by the window. "I think your idea is a great one.

But I don't know that many people who can dance to both hip-hop and swing music. Do you?"

"I can. And I'll bet Justin can too." She looked up at the ceiling. "I imagine Kelsey can. She teaches dance and the yoga, you know, so she can probably do all sorts of things."

Jade mulled this over. Greta did have a point. A dance contest would be fun, and it could bring in people who might not come to the celebration otherwise. She just wondered how many paramedics they should have standing by.

Chapter Eleven

J ADE FUMBLED WITH HER door lock so badly that evening that
Caleb asked for the key and unlocked the door himself.

"Thanks. I…I don't know why I'm so…" She shrugged.
"Butterfingers."

Caleb pushed the door open and allowed Jade to go through
first. The turkey smelled wonderful, and Caleb commented on that.

"It does, doesn't it? I hope it'll taste good. This is my first time
using this recipe."

"It'll be delicious."

Jade had placed the pet carrier on the floor but had neglected to
let Mocha out. Caleb bent and opened the door.

"Oh, my gosh! Yes! Thank you!"

"Jade, why are you so nervous?" Caleb placed his hands on her
waist.

The gesture sent shivers throughout her body. She found it
terrifying as well as exciting. "I don't know. I don't usually do this
type of thing."

"I heard through the grapevine that there's going to be a dance
competition on Saturday." He began to sway slightly, his hands
encouraging her to do so as well.

"Word travels fast."

He nodded. "We don't have much time. We should practice."

"Um, we don't have any music."

Caleb began humming some nonsensical tune.

She laughed. "Why me?"

"Why you? What do you mean? Why are you so unlucky as to have me as a dance partner? Or why are you so lucky as to be the first to hear this as-yet unfinished melody?"

"Guys like you don't date girls like me."

"Apparently they do because here we are."

"Well, it's new for me. I was never popular in high school. My nickname was Jittery Jade because I'd get nervous and embarrassed when a boy paid attention to me."

"High school is a short four years of a person's life. While you're going through it, you feel like it's a lifetime, but it's not. I can't fathom why some people—not you, so don't get huffy with me—get so wrapped up in that time period that they're unable to move on from the persona they developed then."

"Sounds like I hit a nerve."

"Not really," Caleb said. "I dealt with my issues. If I could, I'd go back and tell freshman Caleb that none of the crap he went through then mattered, that it didn't define him." He shrugged. "It took me a little longer to realize that—senior year, as a matter of fact—but I did realize it. That's what's important."

"I...wow. I figured that with your looks, you were the big man on campus at your school."

Caleb resumed humming, but now the tune had words: "Jade thinks I'm handsome. Jade thinks I'm handsome."

Mocha wound around Jade's feet, causing her to stumble against Caleb's broad chest and Caleb to add another verse to his song: "You'd better feed the lion before he kills us. He's a hungry predator."

It was then that Jade realized how Caleb could've been kinda nerdy in high school. But he was perfectly wonderful now, and she'd have thought so then too.

Jade took the turkey out of the slow cooker and, as the recipe instructed, let it rest for twenty minutes. She used this time to playfully slap Caleb's hands away from it, preheat the broiler, and make the gravy. While the turkey was under the broiler "crisping," Jade put the finishing touches on the chocolate peanut butter poke cake.

"Oh, man!" Caleb's fingers strayed toward the icing.

"Don't you dare," she warned.

"Then you'd better give me something to do to keep me away from temptation."

"The sides are in the refrigerator in deli containers. Would you please put them in serving bowls—they're in the cabinet to your left—and warm them up in the microwave?"

"I'm on it." His hand still hovered above the cake. "Just one tiny…"

"Fine," she said.

He grinned, ran his finger through the icing, and moaned with pleasure when he tasted it. That moan did tingly things to Jade's insides. She turned away so Caleb wouldn't see her blush.

It was nice working in the kitchen side by side with Caleb. They made a good team. It was even nicer when they were able to sit down and eat. Jade hadn't realized until that moment how hungry she was. Her day-long battle with nerves meant that she hadn't really eaten anything all day.

"You have a beautiful home," Caleb said, as he cut into a slice of the turkey breast.

"Thank you. It belonged to Grandma. She sold it to me—and threw in most of the stuff you see here for free—when she moved into the Community Center."

"Why'd she decide to make such a big change?"

"I'm not completely sure." Jade sipped her iced tea. "My grandpa died five years ago. They used to do everything together, but when he died, she just kinda quit. She stopped going places, dropped out of groups they'd belonged to, and began staying home a lot more. But, you know, she didn't see that as a problem until Greta was widowed and began doing the same thing."

"It's easier to observe outward than it is to reflect inward, young grasshopper."

She chuckled. "You're so weird."

"But wise."

"Okay, maybe. Anyway, Grandma talked Greta into checking out the Community Center when they did the open house. They both fell in love with it and leased apartments side by side."

"That's really cool. I'm glad the two of them have each other."

"Me too. Greta especially. I mean, Grandma has me and my mom. But when Greta's husband died, she had no one. Well, as far as family members go."

"That's sad. I'd imagine Greta would have made a cool mom."

"She did have a son. He died in a car accident years ago."

"Oh, man. That's terrible. I'm so sorry."

"I am too. Um, not to change the subject—okay, maybe to change the subject—what happened between you and Adalyn?"

Caleb swallowed, took a drink of tea, sat his glass down, and then picked it up and took another drink.

"You really don't want to talk about this, do you?" Jade tore a roll in half while she waited for him to answer. "You don't have to." *You* have to. *Come on. I just want to know the deal. Are you over her? Is there a chance you might get back together? I don't want to put my heart on the line if you're going to hang it out to dry.*

"No, it's fine. It's just a little awkward to discuss with you, that's all." He dabbed at his mouth with his napkin. "Adalyn and I met when we both moved into the Community Center. We started dating. I thought we were keeping everything casual. I mean, as far as I was concerned, we were getting to know each other. Period."

"And she had other ideas?"

"Yeah, she started talking about 'our' future, how many kids she thought we should have, and how much money I thought I'd be making once I graduate next year." He shook his head. "I put the brakes on in a hurry. I realized she was desperate to find someone to take care of her, and I am not that person. I want a partner, not a dependent."

Jade nodded thoughtfully. *Okay. I can live with that. I want a partner too. And two kids—a boy and a girl—would be perfect. But I'm not telling* him *that.*

When they'd finished eating, Caleb helped Jade clean up the kitchen.

"Wait," he said, when she started to blow out the candles. He pulled up a song on his phone and turned up the volume.

Caleb placed the phone on the table and opened his arms. "Dance with me."

Jade walked into his embrace. He took her hand, kissed it, and held it as he danced with her around the kitchen. Jade thought it was the most perfect moment she'd ever experienced. She was wrong. The most perfect moment she'd ever experienced was when he lowered his mouth to kiss her.

Chapter Twelve

❀

MILLIE HAD JUST GOTTEN dressed and had lain back down when her doorbell rang. She dragged herself into a sitting position and ran a hand over her face. She hoped it wasn't someone she'd need makeup to face, but at this time of the day, she doubted it was.

She went to the door and found Jade standing there with a plastic container.

"Good morning, Grandma." She held out the container. "I brought you some chocolate peanut butter poke cake. Have you had breakfast yet?"

Had she? She didn't think so. But she wasn't hungry.

"I'll save this for later. Thank you." She took the container and put it into the refrigerator.

Jade followed her to the kitchen. "Aren't you going to ask why I made a cake?"

"All right. Why did you make a cake?"

"I made dinner for Caleb last night."

"Well, good for you. What did you have besides cake?"

"Turkey breast, rolls, green beans, and mashed potatoes." Jade smiled.

"I'm proud of you." *Maybe not as proud of you as you are of yourself, but I'm proud.*

"Grandma, you look tired."

"I am tired. I think I'll go down to the pharmacy sometime today and get some vitamins. Maybe I've become immune to the ones I've been taking."

Jade frowned. "Can that happen?"

"I don't know. I just know I want to feel better and quit dragging around here like an old woman. Because I'm *not* an old woman."

"I know."

"I'll stop in and see you and Terri at Nothin' But Knit if I make it to the pharmacy."

"If you make it?" Jade's eyes widened.

"Don't worry. I'm not going to keel over. I just meant if I decide to go."

* * *

Jade had already been to Nothin' But Knit before Terri had arrived and had left Mocha there. Normally, she'd have taken him with her to Millie's, but she wanted to put him down and let him get settled. Plus, she'd wanted to put the cake she'd brought for Terri and Caleb in the mini-fridge.

Terri grabbed Jade and squeezed her tightly when she walked into the shop. "I want to hear all about it! Was it wonderful?"

"It was…and I'll get to that in a minute, but I'm worried about Grandma. She's tired, and her color is off. I mean, she didn't have her makeup on—which is unusual for her—but it wasn't that." She raised a thumbnail to her lips, and Terri batted it down. "Thanks. I don't need to take up that bad habit again. She said she might come by here today. If she does, will you inconspicuously watch her and see if you think I'm overreacting?"

"Of course. Now, tell me about that date."

Jade smiled. "It began and ended with a dance."

Terri pretended to swoon onto the counter.

* * *

Millie plodded into Nothin' But Knit about an hour later and sat on the bench by the window. Jade was busy helping a customer learn how to make a broken rib stitch, so Terri went over and sat beside Millie.

"How are you feeling?" Terri asked.

"I'm fine. I'm tired of you and Jade hovering around me as if I'm about to take my last breath. You're like those children in the park with those remote-controlled planes. They fly them too close to you, it's aggravating, and you're itching to swat them down."

"Are you threatening to swat Jade and me?" Terri asked.

"If you don't stop being worrywarts, I just might. Especially Jade. Every time something good happens, she starts looking around for the bad."

"I believe her date with Caleb last night went well."

"Yeah, so do I. But then, in Jade's mind, since that went all right, I must be dying. Well, even if I am, there's not a thing she can do about it, so there." She huffed. "I'm going to the pharmacy and getting some vitamins. Before you know it, I'll be running circles around the both of you."

"Um, Millie...you're holding a bag from the pharmacy."

Millie looked down at the bag. "So I am. I guess I'd better go upstairs and take one of these."

* * *

When Jade's customer left, she came to sit by Terri on the bench her grandmother had so recently vacated.

Terri raised her eyebrows. "I don't know who came in here, but that wasn't our Millie."

"What do you mean?"

"That was a grouchy, addlepated woman." Terri recounted her conversation with Millie and the fact that Millie had talked about needing to go to the pharmacy when the bag she was holding attested to the fact that she'd already been there.

"That's not like her at all. Should I call in the big gun?"

Knowing Jade was talking about her mother, Terri said, "I wouldn't yet. Use that one as a last resort. I'd just keep an eye on Millie today and see if the vitamins do make her feel better."

"Okay. Would you mind holding down the fort while I run a piece of cake over to Caleb? I thought he might want to have it with his lunch."

"Sure, Ms. Any-Excuse-To-See-Him. Take your time."

"It's not an excuse. It's cake. And I brought you some too."

"I do love cake," Terri said.

"I know."

Jade retrieved one of the containers from the refrigerator and took it to Hightail It! She was relieved to see that there weren't any customers in the shop at the moment and that Caleb was standing at the counter.

She held the container aloft. "I brought you some cake."

"Yes." He grinned. "What did I do to score that?"

"Well, for one thing, I know you enjoyed it. And for another, I don't need all that cake around my house."

"Then I'm glad to help you get rid of the cake." He took the container and leaned across the counter to give her a quick peck on the lips. "Thank you."

"I'd better get back."

"Wait. I'd like to return the favor of your making dinner for me last night," Caleb said. "Would you let me cook for you tonight?"

"Okay."

"Do you like spaghetti and meatballs?"

Jade laughed.

"What's funny about spaghetti and meatballs?"

"It's what I was going to make for you, but I didn't know whether you liked it or not."

"Who doesn't like spaghetti and meatballs?" he asked.

"Fair enough. What time?"

"Does right after closing work for you?"

"It does." She headed to the cat food aisle. "But I'd better get Mocha a can of food if I'm not going home first."

Jade was smiling when she all but floated back into Nothin' But Knit.

"Girl, you have it so bad for that man."

"He's making dinner for me tonight after work."

"Ooh la la. You know, you can tell a lot about a man from his apartment." She rubbed her hands together.

"Such as?"

"Lots. Let's just leave it at that. Until tomorrow morning."

Jade fed Mocha and left the cat at Nothin' But Knit. He had a bed and a litterbox there, and he'd be fine until Jade returned for him.

She was nervous as she climbed the stairs to Caleb's apartment. He opened the door and greeted her with a kiss before ushering her inside. She glanced around, remembering Terri's words about being able to tell a lot about a person from his apartment. Right away, she could see that Caleb was tidy. He had a lot of books, and there was also an e-reader on the bookshelf. He had decorated the apartment in lots of dark browns and cream colors. There was a scented candle on the coffee table. She read the label: Oak Aged Whiskey.

"The sauce is simmering, and the meatballs are in the oven," Caleb said. "Where's Mocha?"

"I left him at Nothin' But Knit. He has everything he needs down there, and I didn't want to impose on you."

"Nonsense, go get him."

"Really?"

"Go."

She was glad. *You can also tell a lot about a person from the way he treats your pet.*

When Jade and Mocha returned to Caleb's apartment, he had set the table and was putting the spaghetti into a pot of boiling water.

"Is there anything I can do to help?" Jade asked.

"Actually, there is." He bent his lips to hers. "I needed that."

* * *

Millie was dozing in front of the television when Jade, Caleb, and Mocha paid her a visit. They brought some spaghetti and meatballs for her.

"Have you had dinner yet?" Jade asked.

Had she? She had no idea. She flipped off the television. "No."

"Come on in here to the kitchen, and I'll fix you a plate," Jade said.

Millie got up and went into the kitchen. "What about you?" she asked Caleb. "Have you eaten?"

"Yes. Jade and I just finished dinner. I made enough to feed a village, so we had plenty left over and thought you might enjoy some."

"All right." She sat down at the table, and Jade sat a plate in front of her.

"What would you like to drink, Grandma?"

"I don't care."

"How about tea?"

"Not tea, Jade. It'll keep me up half the night. That's probably why I'm dozing off in the middle of the day—I'm not getting enough sleep at night."

"Okay. Water then."

Jade poured a glass of water and placed it near the plate. She handed Millie a fork and a napkin.

"Are you two going to sit here and watch me eat?" Millie asked. "Go into the living room or something."

"Okaaay." Jade got up, and she and Caleb went to sit on the sofa.

"I'm not a child. I'm tired of people treating me like a child." Millie got up and went down the hall toward the bathroom. She had to take hold of the wall at one point to steady herself.

Millie returned and looked at Caleb and Jade sitting on the sofa. "What are you two doing here? You look like three rainy days." She frowned. "Did something happen to Perry?"

"No, Millie, Perry is doing great," Caleb said.

"Grandma, why don't you let Caleb and me take you to the emergency room?"

"Why would you want to do that? I'm fine."

"But—"

"Jade, I'm fine."

* * *

"Caleb, something's not right," Jade said, in the hallway on the way back to Caleb's apartment. "That's not Grandma. She went to the bathroom and forgot why we were there by the time she got back. That's scary."

"Yeah. I'm worried too."

When they got back to Caleb's apartment, Jade called her mother and asked her to come to the Community Center. She hated to do it, but she felt she was out of options. Fiona was sure Jade was overreacting, but she finally agreed to come and see her mother for herself.

"Do you want me to go with you to see Grandma?" Jade asked.

"No. You've obviously upset her enough for one night."

"Fine. I'll be at Nothin' But Knit when you're finished talking with her." Jade ended the call and turned to Caleb. "I don't want Mocha to go that long without a litterbox."

"I understand. The café is still open, so I'll get us a drink and meet you at the shop. What would you like?"

"An iced green tea would be terrific."

"You've got it."

Jade was sitting on the bench by the window staring down at the floor and worrying that her grandmother was in the first stages of Alzheimer's when Caleb arrived with their drinks. He placed the drinks on the window ledge and put his arm around her. She leaned against him and rested her head against his shoulder.

"Do Millie and your mom have a good relationship?"

"No, but Grandma might agree to go to the doctor simply to shut Mom up."

Caleb chuckled. "That kinda reminds me of my three-year-old niece who was the only person who could make my dad stop smoking."

"How'd she do that?"

"One day, Dad was standing on the porch smoking, and Ellie cried and said Pop Pop was a dragon. She refused to go near him until after he stopped smoking—not just that day, but in general."

"Is Ellie your brother's child or your sister's child?" Jade asked.

"She's my older sister's child. There are only two of us Young children."

Jade smiled.

Mocha hopped up on Jade's lap and lay down. He didn't want to miss out on this window bench love-fest.

About an hour and a half later, Fiona stormed into Nothin' But Knit. Her auburn hair was up in a French twist, she wore a cobalt dress and nude heels, and tonight her eyes were blue. She liked to coordinate her colored contacts—brown, blue, green, and violet—with her outfits.

"Thank you for ruining my evening, Jade. Mom is fine. But if it'll make you happy, I'll call tomorrow morning and make her an appointment with her doctor."

"That would make me ecstatic. Thank you." She held a hand toward Caleb. "Mom, this is Caleb Young. Caleb, this is Fiona

Fairchild." Fiona had always enjoyed being a "fair child" too much to take her husbands' surnames.

"Nice to meet you," said Fiona.

Caleb reached out for a handshake, but Fiona ignored him and left.

"Sorry about that," Jade said.

"Oh, that's all right. She's probably more concerned about Millie than she's letting on."

Jade nodded, but she knew better. That was merely Fiona being Fiona.

She knew her mother loved her…and Fiona loved Grandma too, for that matter. But Fiona was a narcissist. First and foremost, Fiona cared about how things affected her or how they made her look to others. Jade knew that was the main reason Fiona wanted her to have a more prestigious job or an enviable marriage. A high school psychology class had given Jade insight into her mother's personality. It hadn't made the two of them get along any better, but it had helped Jade understand Fiona a little more. These days, Jade gave her mom a pretty wide berth. Less interaction led to more harmonious encounters…usually. Not this time though.

Chapter Thirteen

JADE HAD BEEN AT Nothin' But Knit for nearly half an hour by the time Terri came in. Terri glanced at the clock on the wall behind the counter and asked if she was late.

"No, I got here early." She smiled. "Caleb is the most wonderful guy I've ever met." She told Terri about their date and the fact that he stayed with her until Fiona had gone and checked on Millie.

"Have you been up to check on Millie this morning?"

"No. I wanted to let her sleep in. I thought I'd check on her at lunchtime. Mom said she'd make her an appointment with her doctor this morning. I'm wondering if I should call her and ask if she's done it yet."

"And risk the wrath of Her Highness?" Terri held up her hands. "Better you than me."

Greta flounced into Nothin' But Knit with a cheerful, "Hidey-ho, fam!"

Mocha raced to his bed beneath the counter.

"That's the most jumpy cat I've ever seen," said Greta.

"Good morning, Greta. Have you seen Grandma this morning?"

"Yes, I have, and that woman is tee-totally fit to be tied over you siccing Fiona on her last night."

Jade winced. "I know it was a drastic thing to do, but I was really worried about her."

"I know, hon. I'm just warning you that she's as ornery as a one-toothed junkyard dog trying to gobble down a T-bone." She raised her brows and nodded. "But delivering a warning is not the only reason I'm here. I'm hoping you gals will help with the set-up for the celebration this evening. Can I count on you?"

Both Jade and Terri said they'd be happy to help.

"Thanks. I'm off to see who else I can wrangle into a job."

As soon as Greta was out of earshot, Terri frowned at Jade and asked, "How ornery would a junkyard dog be if he had a steak?"

"Well, he has a steak, but he doesn't have the teeth to adequately eat it…so maybe he's aggravated about that?"

"But he still has a steak. Nobody is trying to take it away from him. So, what do you think this means about Millie's frame of mind this morning?"

"I have no idea what it means about Grandma's state of mind, but I can see that the two of us are giving Greta's whacked-out analogy way too much consideration."

Kelsey sauntered into the shop just before noon. She wore a pink-and-navy crop top and matching yoga pants that came to just below her knees. Her hair fell in soft waves around her shoulders. The young woman was stunning to the point that it made some other women—in this case, Jade—not want to like her, especially when Kelsey flirted with the man those other women were interested in.

Terri, on the other hand, greeted Kelsey as if she were her best friend. "Hi! Welcome to Nothin' But Knit. What brings you by?"

"This is cool." Kelsey gazed around the shop. She strode over to feel some of the yarn in the bins and then spun around to face Terri. "I want you to teach me how to knit. The app said you guys are holding a beginners' class soon?"

"That's right. We are, and we'd love to have you join us," Terri said.

"Great. Is it hard to do?" Kelsey looked at Jade when she was asking, as if afraid Terri would give her the answer she wanted.

She had good instincts.

"Not once you get the hang of it," Jade said. "Why do you want to learn? Is there something specific you'd like to make?"

"I want to make a scarf for Justin." Kelsey's perfectly contoured cheeks pinkened. "I know it's silly, but he's really impressed by all the stuff Greta can do—bake, cook, sew, knit. I think his mom is like a modern-day Martha Stewart or something, so…" She let the thought hang in the air.

"So, you want to show him you're more than a pretty face," Terri said.

"Exactly!" Kelsey grinned at Terri. "I mean, you know."

That was another of Kelsey's sentences she left unfinished because she certainly couldn't honestly deny that she had a pretty face.

"When I saw you and Caleb in the hall the other day, I'd been to see Greta," Kelsey told Jade. "I took her some hibiscus tea, even though she'd told me she didn't need any, because I wanted an excuse to talk with her. Anyway, she's teaching Justin how to cook. But she says she can teach me how to make some dishes she isn't teaching him."

"I wish you luck getting your man," Jade said, "but I have to ask if he's worth everything you're doing."

"Sure, he is." Kelsey smiled. "And even if I don't get the guy, I'm still improving myself. How can that be a bad thing?"

"It can't." Terri handed Kelsey a clipboard holding the form for the beginners' knitting class. "Fill this out, and we'll be in touch a couple of days before the class starts."

"Great! Oh, and Jade?"

Jade turned to Kelsey.

"Don't worry about Adalyn. She posted on social media that her uncle left her some money and that she might stay in South Carolina and sublet her apartment."

Jade knew that news shouldn't affect her in the least. Who cared what Adalyn did? If Jade couldn't land Caleb without worrying that his ex-girlfriend might come between them, then she and Caleb weren't meant to be. Still, she couldn't help but smile.

They closed up Nothin' But Knit that evening, left Mocha lounging on the bench near the window, and wandered to the common area where Sandra and the volunteers were assembling. Neither of them was terribly happy to be among the crowd. Sure, they were eager to help Greta and wanted to see the celebration succeed, but there were so many strangers there.

Gazing around hoping to see a familiar face besides Sandra's, Jade was surprised when someone bumped up against her. She turned and smiled in relief when she saw that it was Caleb.

She gave him a one-armed hug. "I'm so glad you're here."

"I'm glad *you're* here. I went to see Millie on my lunch break. I came up with an excellent excuse." He took his phone from his pocket and pulled up a photo of Perry. "I called the sanctuary and had Keith send me this."

"You're a genius. I didn't have an excuse when I went up at lunchtime, other than to say I was checking on her. That didn't go over well. Mom did make Grandma an appointment with her doctor, but they couldn't work her in until Tuesday."

Greta worked her way through the crowd. "Hidey-ho, kids. I got a call from your grandmother a few minutes ago, Jade. She said she's tuckered out and is going to have to miss out on the fun tonight."

"Do you think I should go up and see about her?" Jade asked.

"Heck, no. I got the emphatic impression that Millie wants to be left alone tonight."

For the next few hours, everyone worked to get tables set up, banners hung, signs printed out and placed, and flyers made with events and times. Every once in a while, Jade would see Caleb, and he'd give her a wink and a smile.

Once all the work had been completed, the group of volunteers gathered in the café.

Greta hurried over to Jade and Terri. "Look! No, not like that. Don't be so obvious about it. Mitch Reedy is over there talking with Sandra." She took out her makeup bag and thrust her purse toward Terri. "Hold this a second, would you?" She carefully reapplied her mauve lipstick. "How's that?"

"You look terrific," Terri said.

"Thanks." She grabbed her purse with one hand and Terri's arm with the other. "Let's get over there."

Jade was watching Terri and Greta infiltrate the interview when Caleb came up and slid an arm around her waist.

"Hi," she said with a smile.

"Hi. Let's grab a booth before it gets too crowded in here."

She nodded toward the TV crew. "Hopefully, we'll get one where we can see the show."

"Nothing like dinner theater."

Both Jade and Caleb were surprised that when the camera was turned on Greta, she handled the interview like a pro. She invited everyone out for a wonderful day of fun for the entire family and even flirted a little bit with Mitch Reedy. Terri, on the other hand, stammered and flushed and looked terrified.

"Oh, no," Jade whispered. "Terri bombed."

"That's all right," Caleb said. "They can fix that in the editing room."

"I doubt they can fix *that*."

Upon finishing her interview, Terri slid into the booth across from Jade and put her head in her hands. "Mitch Reedy must think I'm an idiot."

"Scooch over," Greta said.

Terri made room for Greta, and the older woman sat beside her.

"Do you feel like Mitch Reedy thinks I'm an idiot?" Terri asked.

"He probably does," Greta said.

Jade's jaw dropped.

"But I'm gonna work with you so that after tomorrow he won't," Greta finished. "He'll be impressed with you."

Terri lifted her head. "He's never going to give me another chance to be on TV after I botched that."

"Well, there is that." Greta tilted her head. "Maybe he will. I'll see if I can get you in. But, even if you don't get on the news, I thought you were trying to impress the *man*, not the *public*."

When Terri was silent, Jade asked, "Greta, how did you get to be so comfortable in front of a television camera?"

"In my younger days, I did commercials for local businesses, mainly for car dealerships. For one place, the slogan was, 'We love to drive, and it shows.'"

A golden oldie—a man whose name Jade couldn't recall because she'd only met him when they'd started working that evening—turned around and said to Greta, "Hey, I thought that slogan belonged to Delta. You know, 'We love to *fly*, and it shows.'"

"Yeah, it did. The dealership eventually got in trouble over that, and I had to quit saying it. I was pretty much out of the commercial business after that."

Chapter Fourteen

JADE AND TERRI HAD worked it out before leaving the café Friday night that they'd take turns running the shop and checking out the celebration on Saturday. Most of the volunteers working the events were golden oldies or YPs who worked somewhere other than the Kinsey Falls Living and Retail Community Center.

During their first two hours of work, they were both so busy neither of them could leave. But when they finally got a lull, Terri encouraged Jade to go check everything out.

"No," said Jade. "You go first."

"I want to wait here in case Mitch Reedy comes by. Greta worked with me last night, and I think I'll do better if he interviews me again."

"All right, then. If you're sure."

"I'm sure." Terri waved her hands as if she were shooing Jade out the door.

"I'll be back in thirty minutes, tops."

When Jade stepped out of Nothin' But Knit, the smell of kettle corn welcomed her. She looked to her right and spotted the popcorn cart. She wandered over and bought a small bag. She then moved slightly away from everything so she could munch her kettle corn and see what she'd like to do before going back to relieve Terri.

One of the authors had a book whose cover was particularly intriguing. Jade had decided to walk over and see what the book was about when she heard a male voice say, "Jade Burt? Is that you?"

She turned. Her stomach dropped, and she had to clutch the bag she was holding to keep from letting it spill onto the floor.

"Blake." Her empty hand clenched into a fist. "Wh-what are you doing here?"

Jade's mind flashed back to that long-ago scene in the hallway where this guy standing next to her so casually today told her that he'd take her to the dance if she made him keep his word. She wished he'd gotten fat or gone bald or grew a wart on his nose. But, no, he looked exactly the same—same longish black hair, same blue eyes, same solid, athletic build.

Oddly, though, his looks didn't affect her the way they had when she was in high school. He wasn't as handsome as she'd always thought he was. Even after he'd humiliated her, she'd still thought he *looked* dreamy. Yes, he was a jerk, but a handsome jerk.

"I just thought I'd check this place out," Blake was saying now.

She forced her mind to fully return to the present.

"I've been kinda looking for a new apartment," he said. "Do you live here?"

"No," Jade said. "I have a store here."

"Really? Cool. Which one?"

"Nothin' But Knit."

His eyes raked over her. "You haven't changed a bit. You're still as pretty as you were in high school, maybe even more so."

It took all of Jade's willpower not to throw the bag of kettle corn at him. What did he think—that she'd stand there and fawn all over him because he called her pretty? Did he think she'd forgotten how he'd treated her in high school?

"You and I never did go on a date, did we?"

Jade clenched her teeth, her face burning with anger and shame. She had to keep her fury under control. She couldn't lash out at him and make a scene. It was bad enough that he'd ruined her high school years. She wasn't about to let him ruin Nothin' But Knit and the Community Center for her too.

At that moment, Caleb came up holding a tiny blue bandana with Hightail It! Kinsey Falls written on it. "Hi, babe." He kissed her on the cheek before handing her the bandana. "This is for Mocha."

Jade threw her arms around him and kissed him passionately on the lips.

"Wow. I'll bring things to Mocha more often." He grinned. "You think he'll like it?"

She laughed. "He'll hate it."

"Will you put it on him and take a photo anyway?"

"Of course. He can stand it for that long."

"Good." Caleb turned and held out his hand. "Caleb Young. Sorry for interrupting."

Blake shook Caleb's hand and introduced himself.

"I always welcome an interruption from you," Jade told Caleb.

"I need to be going," Blake said. "Good seeing you, Jade."

Jade gave him a brief nod.

As soon as Blake walked away, Caleb said, "I am sorry for intruding, but you looked awfully uncomfortable. I wanted to give you an out if you needed one."

"I definitely needed one. Thank you for coming to my rescue."

"Anytime. Did I mention that the bandana I gave you is for Mocha? That seemed to get quite a reaction last time."

Jade stood on her tiptoes and kissed him on the lips.

"Hmm. Nice, but I guess I'll have to come up with a new gesture to get another kiss like that first one."

"I'm saving it for later," Jade said. "You're my hero."

Caleb grinned. "I like the sound of that." He stole a handful of popcorn. "I hope to collect on that kiss later."

"Oh, you will."

Jade hurried back to Nothin' But Knit, but Terri was with a customer. Jade put the bandana in her purse and stuffed her purse under the counter. As she did so, an older woman and a little girl came up to the counter with several skeins of yarn and some knitting needles.

"I'm going to teach my granddaughter how to knit," said the older woman, smiling broadly.

"That's wonderful." Jade looked at the granddaughter. "I love to knit."

"I think I'm going to love it too."

As soon as the traffic lightened but before Terri could take off to explore the festivities, Jade asked her, "Guess who I ran into in the hall? Maybe 'ran into' isn't the best term because he came right over to me and said 'hello.'"

"Who?"

"Blake." Jade folded her arms over her chest.

"Blake from high school?" Terri gasped. "Are you serious? Did he apologize for treating you like crap back then?"

"No, but he did tell me that he and I never did get to go on a date."

Terri narrowed her eyes. "That skunk. What did you say?"

"I didn't have to say anything. There I am, wishing the floor would open up and swallow me—or him—when Caleb comes up and kisses me on the cheek."

"I love it," Terri said. "Although I do kinda wish he'd kissed you on the lips."

"Well, I took care of that."

Terri gaped. "You did not!"

Jade giggled. "I did. I kissed that man like there was no tomorrow."

"I'm proud of you." Terri laughed. "That's so perfect. Did Caleb just happen to be passing by or what?"

"He said I looked uncomfortable and thought I might need rescuing."

Terri placed her hand over her heart. "Oh, Jade, that guy is such a keeper. Does he have a brother?"

"Sorry, no. But I know there's a wonderful guy out there for you too."

"Yeah, easy for you to say."

"Hidey-ho!" Greta came through the door with arms wide. "I'm embracing life today. And so are you, Terri. Come on. We're going to do some vocal exercises and hopefully get you another interview. Mercifully, they cut you out of last night's clip."

* * *

Millie was practically giddy when she sauntered into Nothin' But Knit later that day. She fluttered a piece of paper at Jade. "Look what I got."

Jade moved closer. "What is it?"

"It's a fifty-dollar gift certificate to the salon. I won it playing bingo."

"Congratulations." Jade hugged her. "I wonder who'll win our gift basket."

"I don't know, but the bingo room is packed. If you get a chance, you should go up there."

"I will, though I doubt I'd win anything. I never do."

"Don't be such a negative Nellie," Millie said. "By the way, I'm sorry I was so grouchy last night. I haven't been feeling up to par, and it's probably good that I'm going to the doctor on Tuesday to get checked out." She looked around the shop. "Where's Mocha?"

"I was afraid all the extra traffic in and out of here would stress him out, so I left him at home today."

"That was probably wise."

"Are you going to participate in the dance competition tonight?"

Millie laughed. "No, but I wouldn't miss it for anything. This morning, Greta showed me part of the hip-hop dance routine Kelsey taught her." She shook her head. "I got a load of the outfit she's wearing for it too—a baseball cap to be worn backward, baggy jeans, high-top sneakers. She's ready."

"I'm sure she is. I'm really glad the shops are closing in time for the dance competition. I can hardly wait to see Greta compete. Does she have a partner?"

"As far as I know, she's going it alone," Millie said. "And if anyone laughs at her, I'm going to smack 'em. I mean, if I can wait until I get home to giggle, everyone else can too."

* * *

When Terri returned, she was unable to keep a smile off her face. Jade watched her, but Terri simply put her head down and went around helping customers until the store was empty.

Seeing her chance, Jade asked, "What's going on?"

"Mitch Reedy interviewed me again. And this time, Jade, I did really well. Plus—are you ready for this?"

"I'm ready! Spill it!"

"He asked me to have lunch with him tomorrow."

"Who did?"

"Mitch Reedy!"

"Channel 10's very own man in the field, Mitch Reedy?"

"Yes! That Mitch Reedy."

Jade laughed. "I'm happy for you. I hope the two of you hit it off."

"So do I." She shrugged. "But, you know, I'm not expecting anything other than a nice lunch."

"Uh huh. Is the camera crew still here?"

"No, why?" Terri asked. "Did you want to make an announcement?"

114

"No, I just wondered if they'd be here for the dance competition. I hear that Greta is going to put on a one-woman show that might bring the house down."

It was standing room only when Terri and Jade arrived at the dance competition. They stood in the back of the room and looked to see if they could pick out anyone they knew. Caleb was standing beside Millie, and when he caught Jade's eye, he motioned for her and Terri to join them.

Several couples and groups had entered the contest to perform to music from different decades. One pair wore twenties-style clothing and danced the Charleston. Another couple performed the jitterbug. A golden oldie couple danced a lovely tango.

And then it was Greta's turn. Her outfit was every bit as wild as Millie had promised it would be, and Jade covered her mouth with her hand to help stifle a giggle. She didn't want Millie smacking her before Greta even got started.

Although Greta might have intended to do a solo act, when she went out onto the stage, the lights dimmed, a number of spotlights danced across the floor, and Kelsey and several willowy young women joined her. Jade thought it must be one of Kelsey's dance classes, and they were there acting as Greta's backup dancers.

How cool is that? Her estimation of Kelsey skyrocketed.

The crowd cheered as Greta and her dance troop popped and locked, dubstepped, and grooved.

"She looks amazing out there," Terri shouted to Jade.

"I know!"

"Jade," Caleb said.

She turned to look at him. He was staring at Millie, whose head was bobbing. Millie started to fall forward, but Caleb caught her.

Jade began looking toward the back of the room. She knew Sandra had insisted on having EMTs at the Community Center throughout the day.

"Come on," she said to Caleb.

"Oh, my gosh." Terri's face had lost its color.

"Don't you faint on us too."

"What do you need me to do?" she asked, falling into step beside Jade.

"Just stay here. I'll call you when I know something."

Caleb rushed through the crowd where the paramedics were standing.

"What happened?" one of them asked.

"She passed out."

"I'm fine," Millie said, though her weak voice argued otherwise. "I just got lightheaded."

The paramedic instructed Caleb to place Millie on a stretcher. Another one slipped a blood pressure cuff onto her arm. After a few minutes, the paramedics determined that Millie should be seen at the ER. She disagreed but didn't have it in her to put up much of an argument.

Chapter Fifteen

CALEB DROVE JADE TO the hospital. She called Fiona while they were on their way. Fiona didn't answer, so Jade left her a voicemail message: "Mom, the paramedics are taking Grandma to the hospital. I don't know what's wrong with her, but you need to go to the emergency room when you get this message."

They arrived at the hospital right behind the ambulance. Caleb let her out so she could go in and be with Millie, and he parked the car.

Jade was standing by the gurney holding Millie's hand when the doctor came in. A nurse was already present, making the room crowded. The doctor asked her to leave while he examined Millie.

"I'll be out to talk with you in a few minutes."

Caleb found Jade standing in the hallway.

"The doctor is in with her," she told him.

"That was quick."

"I know," Jade said. "That's what scares me."

When the doctor emerged from the emergency bay, he told Jade and Caleb that he was fairly certain that Millie was suffering from a urinary tract infection.

"Wait, what?" Jade asked. "That doesn't make any sense. She's confused and tired, and she passed out. She never said she had any urinary tract symptoms."

"In an older adult, a UTI can present non-classic symptoms such as agitation, lethargy, decreased mobility, and decreased appetite," the doctor said.

"What's going on?" Fiona blew through the hallway looking as if she'd stepped out of a hospital scene in a soap opera. "Where's my mother?"

Jade introduced her mother to the doctor.

"Well," he said, "I'm extremely busy. Jade can explain to you what we suspect, and if you have any questions, I'll answer them when I come back."

He left Fiona standing there with her mouth opening and closing like that of a fish. He was apparently not taken by her violet contacts and matching silk blouse. Jade felt a perverse sense of satisfaction about that.

"Mom, they're going to do some lab work to see if Grandma has a UTI."

Fiona ignored her daughter and looked at Caleb. "What are *you* doing here?"

"I brought Jade to the hospital."

"Well, you can go now," Fiona said. "I'm here now. I'll take her home."

"I'd prefer to wait and find out the results of Millie's tests," Caleb said.

Fiona opened her mouth, but before she could say anything else, Jade cut her off.

"Thank you, Caleb. I appreciate that." Jade gave her mother a pointed look.

"Fine." Fiona rummaged through her purse and brought out some crumpled bills. She shoved the bills at Caleb. "Here. Would you please see if you can find a vending machine with some coffee?"

"Sure." Caleb walked off, trying to smooth the bills as he went.

"Why is he here?" Fiona hissed.

"He told you why—he's here with me. Besides, he caught Grandma and kept her from falling."

"I'm grateful for that, but that doesn't mean he has to stick around."

"He cares about Grandma," Jade said, "And he has every right to be here."

"No, he doesn't. The only people who should be here right now are members of our family. He's not family."

"Caleb is very important to me, Mom, and he can stay as long as he wants."

"Are you involved with that man?" Fiona asked.

"Yes."

Fiona pressed her lips together. "He's all wrong for you. You *have* to know that."

Caleb returned and caught the end of Fiona's rant. He handed the bills back to Fiona. "The machine is out of order."

Fiona huffed. "Lovely. I'm going to find someone who can help me out." She stormed off down the hall.

Caleb kissed Jade on the forehead. "Since your mom is here with you, I'm going to take off. Call if you need anything."

"Won't you please wait?"

He shook his head. "I'll check on Millie tomorrow. I'm beat."

When Fiona returned to find Jade in tears, she placed her perfectly manicured hand at her throat. "Is it Mom? Has something happened?"

"No. *You* happened. You might've succeeded in driving away the best thing that ever happened to me."

"Don't be so dramatic," Fiona said.

"Do you want to wait with Grandma, or do you want me to?"

"Why can't we both?"

"Because I don't want to be anywhere near you right now," Jade said.

"Fine. I'll be in the lobby. By myself."

"Good."

The doctor confirmed that Millie was suffering from a UTI. He said they were going to give her one bag of intravenous antibiotics, give her a prescription for some antibiotics in tablet form (after confirming that Millie had no problem swallowing pills), and then Millie could go home. He instructed her to keep the appointment with her doctor on Tuesday.

"By then, we'll know more about your infection and can send the information to your doctor. I'll send the nurse in to finish up with you."

Jade sent a text to Caleb confirming Millie's diagnosis and passing along what the doctor had said. She didn't receive a response. Maybe he'd gone to sleep. Or maybe he'd decided he didn't need to be involved with a woman who had a mother like Fiona.

It was a quiet ride to the Kinsey Falls Living and Retail Community Center. Although she knew her grandmother was exhausted, Jade guessed she was wondering why everyone was silent. Hopefully, Millie thought everyone was tired. She figured Millie had guessed that Jade and Fiona had argued since that was always a safe bet, but it was even more likely in times of crisis.

They arrived at the Community Center at two a.m.

"You should both stay with me," Millie said. "I don't want you driving at this time of night. It's dangerous."

"I'll be okay," said Jade. "I need to go home and take care of Mocha." She kissed Millie on the cheek and told her she'd see her tomorrow.

At about ten a.m., Jade was awakened by a knock on her front door. As she grabbed a robe and went to answer it, she thought it had better not be Fiona. If it was, Jade wouldn't be responsible for her actions.

120

She flung open the door.

Caleb stood there with coffee and a pastry bag from the Community Center café.

Jade blew out a breath, took the coffees and placed them on the hall table, and threw her arms around Caleb's neck. "Thank you."

"It's only coffee and pastries." He wrapped his arms around her.

"Not for that. Thank you for being here. I was afraid Mom had run you off."

"I'm not that easy to get rid of," he said. "I left so your mom would stop yelling and making a scene in the ER. Neither you nor Millie needed that."

Jade kissed him. "I realize we've only had a couple of dates, but I feel like we have a real connection. I'd like to explore that further."

Caleb smiled. "I couldn't have said it better myself."

Epilogue

JADE, CALEB, AND MILLIE were on their way to see Perry the Possum be released back into the wild with his pal, Parker. Caleb drove, with Jade in the passenger seat of his Jeep holding his hand and Millie in the back. Thankfully, she'd fully recovered from her UTI and had her now ever-present water bottle in the cup holder next to her. Her doctor had stressed hydration, and Millie had vowed to do whatever it took to avoid another UTI.

Stealing a glance at Caleb's profile, Jade reflected on how far she'd come in the past six weeks—and how far she and Caleb had come. Once Jade had finally been able to shed her fear and take a chance on their relationship, she'd never been happier. They'd even finally professed their love for each other last week. Jade had been feeling it for longer than that, but after Caleb had spoken about Adalyn getting too clingy too fast, she'd waited until he'd confessed his feelings before giving voice to her own.

She'd even asked Caleb, "Are you sure you don't feel that we're moving too fast?"

He'd said, "Fast is fine when it's the right person."

Jade was shaken out of her reverie when Millie said, "Now that Greta has shown the world she can dance a little bit, I believe she's got her sights set on becoming a detective."

"Now that you mention it, Joanne—the girl who won the Nothin' But Knit basket at the grand opening celebration—told me that Greta was looking at her funny the other day when they were both in the shop." Jade laughed. "Joanne doesn't *look* like a criminal mastermind, but I guess if she is, she won't be able to hide it from Greta."

"That wild woman is going to be the death of all of us," Millie said. "Just you wait and see."

"Nah," Caleb said. "She livens things up."

And then, they were at the wildlife refuge and sanctuary. Keith and Geri had already loaded the possums into the van. Keith motioned for Caleb to follow them.

The three of them could barely contain their excitement as they followed the white van to a remote wooded spot where Perry and Parker were to be released. As instructed, Caleb stopped the Jeep a few feet away from the van. He got out and helped Millie from the backseat. He kept her hand firmly in the crook of his elbow as he brought Millie around to the front of the van to stand with Jade.

Geri got a cage out of the van and carried it into the clearing. She opened the door of the cage and backed away from it.

Two possums scrambled out of the cage and waddled into the field.

"Wonder which one's Perry?" Caleb whispered.

"Perry's in the front," Millie said. "I'd know that little pink nose anywhere."

Coming Soon from
Grace Abraham Publishing

Putting Down Roots in Kinsey Falls (Book Two in the *Kinsey Falls* Series): Joanne Faraday is looking for her biological family. She was adopted at birth and has discovered that her mother died a couple of years after she was born. No father was listed on Joanne's birth certificate. Her mother's last known residence was Kinsey Falls, Virginia. Determined to find her biological father, she takes a job in the pharmacy within the Kinsey Falls Living and Retail Community Center and moves into one of the young professional micro-apartments to conduct her search.

Seeing Joanne "messing where she shouldn't be" in the business center, golden oldie resident Greta Parks is certain that girl is up to something. Is she a terrorist? A spy? After following her around like Jessica Fletcher until Greta annoys her to no end, Joanne confesses what she's doing so Greta will leave her alone. But Greta is like a dog with a brand new bone. She'll be happy to help Joanne track down her biological father. When Greta realizes her late son dated Joanne's mother, her hopes soar. Could Joanne be her granddaughter? Or was Joanne's father the late husband of another of the LRCC residents? The truth could tear them all apart.

(Unedited) Sneak Peek!

"That one right there is up to something." Greta placed a hand on her best friend Millie's arm to halt their approach to Nothin' But Knit.

"Ever since you started reading those cozy mysteries, you've thought everyone was up to something," Millie said.

"Well, she really is. She might look all sweet and charming with that long blonde hair and that girl-next-door smile, but she doesn't have me fooled." Greta nodded. "She's hiding something. I'm sure of it."

Nothin' But Knit was the knitting shop owned by Millie's granddaughter Jade and Jade's friend Terri. The young woman who was "up to something" was standing at the counter with her back to the women.

"What makes you so certain?" Millie asked.

"I went into the business center the other day, and she immediately opened a new tab on the computer she was at. She was looking at something, and she didn't want me to know what it was."

"Maybe—and this is a long shot—it wasn't any of your business."

"It was too my business! What if she's a spy or a terrorist? You just never know these days." Greta shook her head. "But whatever it is, rest assured that Greta Parker is on the case, and I will not rest until I find out what that girl is hiding."

* * *

Joanne Faraday stood at the counter at Nothin' But Knit waiting for the yarn winder to finish spinning the skein of yarn she'd purchased into a ball. She watched Jade's face as the young red-haired woman frowned past Joanne's right shoulder.

"She's behind me, isn't she?" Joanne asked.

"Who?" Jade asked, directing her gaze back at Joanne.

126

"The crazy woman with the plum-colored hair who's been stalking me for the past two days."

Jade smiled. "That's Greta, and she's heading this way with my grandmother Millie. Greta can be a little eccentric, but I think you'll like her when you get to know her."

Joanne wasn't so sure.

The two women entered the shop.

"Hi," Jade said, brightly. "I'd like you guys to meet Joanne Faraday. Joanne, this is my grandmother Millie and her friend Greta."

"Nice to meet you." Joanne could certainly see the resemblance between Jade and Millie. Although Millie's hair was a silvery white, the two shared the same beautiful bone structure. Joanne felt a pang. She'd been adopted as a baby and had no idea who she might look like.

"What brings you guys to the shop?" Jade asked. Millie wasn't a knitter, but she came to check on Jade and Terri often. Greta *was* a knitter, so the two of them seldom came into the shop together.

"Greta was heading this way, and I thought I'd join her and ask if you and Caleb would like to join me for dinner and a movie tonight—my treat."

"I'd planned to go with Millie, but something came up." Greta ventured a glance toward Terri, who was restocking the yarn bins. Terri was poking yarn into the cubbies.

"That sounds great, Grandma," Jade said. "I'll check with Caleb to make sure that works for him." Jade turned to Joanne. "It's actually because of Grandma that my boyfriend and I met." She laughed. "Sometimes, I think he likes her as much as he does me."

"Pish posh," Millie said.

"That's tellin' 'em," Greta said.

Joanne's yarn finished winding, and Jade took the ball off the spool. She handed the yarn to Joanne, who thanked her, and said, "Back to the knitting room."

"I have a lightweight shawl I'd like to work on," Greta said.

127

Joanne wished she hadn't mentioned the knitting room. She supposed she could simply put away her things and leave, but she didn't want to. She wanted to work on her scarf.

"I can get that for you," Terri told Greta. She went into the knitting room, where there were sixteen cabinets. Most of the cabinets were labeled with the names of regular customers who liked to keep projects in the cabinets when they weren't working on them. For residents of the Kinsey Falls Living and Retail Community Center, it helped keep their micro-apartments from getting cluttered with works in progress.

"I believe I'll sit here with you." Greta smiled at Joanne.

There was no one else seated at the table, so she could have sat somewhere other than right next to Joanne, but why would Joanne have expected Greta to sit anywhere else?

###

Author's Notes

Wynnwood Wildlife Rehabilitation

Wynnwood Wildlife Rehabilitation holds state and federal permits and is dedicated to the care and rehabilitation of orphaned and injured wildlife and their return to their natural habitat. The refuge provides food, medical care, housing, therapy, and TLC to a variety of animals. They do so at their own expense. Donations are greatly appreciated and are tax deductible under IRS Code 501(c)(3).

Visit them online at https://www.facebook.com/Wynnwood-Wildlife-Rehabilitation-346890465568/

Wynnwood Wildlife Rehab is an Amazon Smile charity.

Virginia Opossums

Although we Virginians colloquially call our opossums "possums," Perry and Parker are Virginia opossums. Virginia opossums are commonly called North American opossums and are the only marsupials found north of Mexico. They're fascinating little beasties—I didn't realize how much so until I researched them for this book.

I got the idea for Millie finding a possum from real life. One day, my children were playing in the front yard when a large, white possum came waddling through with her back full of babies. One of the babies fell off. I freaked out because I didn't want the baby possum to be attacked by the cats or dogs around, so I got the poor little thing up on a shovel and placed it under a bush where I thought the mother would find and retrieve it. [I have since learned that the mother doesn't come back for babies who fall off her back. She's not even aware she lost them. *sniff*]

Then I called 9-1-1.

"Hello, what is your emergency?"

"Um, there's a…possum…walking through our yard."

"That does not constitute an emergency. You'll need to call animal control."

"I was afraid it might be rabid."

More firmly: "You'll need to call animal control."

I called animal control.

The animal control officer told me that if a nocturnal animal is out during the day with its babies, it's likely not rabid but is simply foraging for food. [I didn't know it at the time, of course, but the low body temperature of opossums makes it rare for them to get rabies at all, and they are immune to most snake venoms.]

Since neither 9-1-1 nor animal control could offer me any assistance, I called my husband.

"What're we gonna do?" I wailed.

"Let nature take its course."

Gasp

He knows me better than that! I never let nature take its course! I once saved a baby bunny from the jaws of the neighbor's cat and then slept in the den with the bunny in a basket during the night—and couldn't find it the next morning. But I digress...that's a story for a different book.

When my husband came home for lunch, I took him to the possum hideout.

"Look at it. It's so sweet!"

"No, it's not."

Glare "It *is* sweet!"

"Fine. What are you going to do with it?"

"Take it to a possum whisperer, I guess."

Sigh *Head Shake* *Goes back to work*

Not long after my husband got back to work, he called me. A woman he worked with wanted to take custody of the possum (by this time, the children and I had named the tiny creature "Hissy" because it hissed at us). I looked for something in which to transport baby Hissy, and I found...a Styrofoam cooler. I know that sounds bad, but it was all I had.

When Hubby got home, we got Hissy into the cooler (once again, gently using the shovel) and put the lid on it. Everyone piled into the car, and off we went to Hubby's office where the woman who raised sugar gliders and wanted to rescue Hissy waited. [One side note: we had to drive through the local country club to get to Hubby's office, which made me laugh because it looked as if we were making a food delivery to the Beverly Hillbillies!]

The woman took Hissy, and Hissy lived for a little while…but, sadly, not for long. Geri from Wynnwood said it probably didn't get the nutrients it needed.

So, the moral of this story is that if you find injured or abandoned wildlife, see if there's a licensed wildlife rehabilitator in your area. If so, take your critter there. It'll appreciate it.

Acknowledgements

Thanks so much to Geri and Keith Wynn of Wynnwood Wildlife Rehabilitation (web address above) for showing me around their facility and educating me (and people in our region) about wildlife rehabilitation. Any mistakes I've made about wildlife rehab in the book are entirely my own. These people know what they're doing. No possums were harmed in the making of this book. I do, however, have a plush one named Perry that sits atop my desk now.

Thank you, Lianna Trent, for being such a talented and observant beta reader! Your suggestions made this book so much better.

Thank you, Jeni Chappelle, for editing under pressure. Great job! (http://www.jenichappelle.com)

Thank you, Mark and Lorna from Author Packages (http://www.authorpackages.com), for the cover, the book formatting, and the hand-holding. It's hard to hold one's hand when you're on another continent, but you did so beautifully!

Recipes

Slow Cooker Turkey Breast
www.recipetineats.com/juicy-slow-cooker-turkey-breast/

Chocolate Peanut Butter Poke Cake
https://www.bettycrocker.com/recipes/peanut-butter-chocolate-poke-cake/6c878f1b-d30c-4cc2-aed1-f56130ada084

About the Author

Gayle Leeson is a pseudonym for Gayle Trent. I also write as Amanda Lee. As Gayle Trent, I write the Daphne Martin Cake Mystery series and the Myrtle Crumb Mystery series. As Amanda Lee, I write the Embroidery Mystery series.

The cake decorating series features a heroine who is starting her life over in Southwest Virginia after a nasty divorce. The heroine, Daphne, has returned to her hometown of Brea Ridge to open a cake baking and decorating business and is wrestling with the question of whether or not one can go home again. She enjoys spending time with her sister, nephew, and niece, but she and her mother have a complicated relationship that isn't always pleasant. Daphne has also reconnected with her high school sweetheart and is pursuing a rekindled romance while desperately trying to put her past behind her.

Kerry Vincent, Hall of Fame Sugar Artist, Oklahoma State Sugar Art Show Director, and Television Personality says the series is "a must read for cake bakers and anyone who has ever spent creative time in the kitchen!"

Says Dean Koontz, #1 New York Times bestselling author, "One day I found myself happily reading . . . mysteries by Gayle Trent. If she can win me over . . . she's got a great future."

The Embroidery Mystery series features a heroine who recently moved to the Oregon coast to open an embroidery specialty shop. Marcy Singer left her home in San Francisco, along with the humiliation of being left at the altar, in order to move to Tallulah Falls and realize her dream of owning her own shop. She takes along her faithful companion, a one-year-old Irish wolfhound named Angus O'Ruff. She makes many new friends in Tallulah Falls, but she also makes a few enemies. Thankfully, her best friend Sadie MacKenzie and her husband Blake run the coffeehouse right down the street from Marcy's shop, the Seven-Year Stitch; and Detective Ted Nash always has her back.

Publishers Weekly says, "Fans of the genre will take kindly to Marcy, her Irish wolfhound, Angus O'Ruff, and Tallulah Falls. This is a fast, pleasant read with prose full of pop culture references and, of course, sharp needlework puns."

Pat Cooper of RT Book Reviews says, "If her debut here is any indication, Lee's new series is going to be fun, spunky and educational. She smoothly interweaves plot with her character's personality and charm, while dropping tantalizing hints of stitching projects and their history. Marcy Singer is young, fun, sharp and likable. Readers will be looking forward to her future adventures." (RT Book Reviews nominated The Quick and the Thread for a 2010 Book Reviewers' Choice Award in the Amateur Sleuth category)

I live in Virginia with my family, which includes my own "Angus" who is not an Irish wolfhound but a Great Pyrenees who provides plenty of inspiration for the character of Mr. O'Ruff. I'm having a blast writing this new series!

The Kinsey Falls series is a departure from the cozy mysteries most of my readers know me for, but I wanted to write a character-driven series that didn't always focus on murders. Don't despair if you prefer the mysteries though! I'm currently at work on a new cozy series called The Ghostly Fashionista Mystery Series. That series features a designer of retro fashions whose studio comes with its own vintage ghost—a woman who died in 1930. Stay tuned…

Please visit me online: https://linktr.ee/gayletrentleeson

Printed in Great Britain
by Amazon

39040189R00079